The Mad Pit

By

Sarah McNeill

I dedicate this book to Philip and my father, Gordon, who was the first to read my tale to the bitter end.

The Staff

Janet Sowerby - Library Operations Manager

Lupin Lawson - Library Floor Manager

Tristan Pear - Archivist

Pete Burrows - Apprentice

The Players

Courtney Harrison - Library user

Ernie Noble - Library user

Bev Rogers - Library user

Stan Tweddle - Library user

Violet Holt - Library user

Helen Jameson - Library user

Tina Jackson - Library user

Malcolm McDonald - Library user

Maeve Mills - Library cleaner

Hazel Wilcox - Library user

Eileen Cannon - Owner of 'The La'al Teacake

The Public Servants

Councillor Norman Roach - Seatown Council

Ian Nicholson - Seatown Council staff officer

Pauline Graves - Director of Community Service

Amanda Love - Community Services Manager

Barry Morgan Amanda's personal assistant

The Others

Gavin McKenna - Seatown Chronicle journalist

Teresa Hibbert - Seatown Chronicle photographer

Bert Braithwaite - Lupin's neighbour

Aiden Lawson - Lupin's father

Anna Lawson - Lupin's mother

Geraldine Simcox - Lupin's fortune teller

Reverend Nixon - St. John's Church of England

Louise Larmour - Sheltering Oaks

Chapter One

Maeve swept her fuzzy duster over the bodice rippers, then lightly tickled the large print.

A huge pair of headphones hugged a compact head of bright blonde frizzy hair.

Today she was listening to the 'Bad Bi%#h Revolutionaries' podcast.

Maeve had big plans.

———————————— *** ————————————

Draining her sugary coffee, Janet watched as the old man dragged his black bin bag into the Madeleine Pit library, affectionately known to the locals as the Mad Pit.

She placed her mug on top of the help desk, turned and stage whispered into the staff kitchen: "Ernie's here and he's been through Tesco's bins."

Lupin sank back into her chair, closed her eyes and commenced a relaxing series of short inhalations followed by long, drawn out breaths. She felt a bit dizzy, and wasn't sure whether to blame her lung capacity, (roll-up ciggies), or Ernie's signature Monday morning stench, (Tesco bins).

"I can't be near that man today," she wheezed. "I was up past midnight moon bathing my new crystals and right now, body and mind is spent."

"You should have gone to your bed and left the stones," Janet said, feeling around the desk for her specs.

"They've just moved house," Lupin huffed. "I had to keep them company."

Janet put on her glasses and strode into the kitchen, filling the space with a delicately styled cloud of blonde bob upon which rested a shimmering hairspray dew. Her eyes swooped over the tiny room and fell upon a rusted tin of air freshener perched on top of the microwave.

"Never mind your shiny pebbles Lup; go and grab the Febreze and remember, this country will never forget your sacrifice."

Lupin slipped the can up her sleeve and tiptoed over the worn red carpet tiles, ready for combat.

"Be discreet, my love," Janet warned, as the Library's premier wiccan swooshed the potent cotton fresh scent under and around the arse of Madeleine Pit library's most unique service user, Ernie.

 ***

"Morning, our Ernie, what're you up to with that bag?" Janet enquired. She'd grown tired of this weekly conversation but wouldn't let on. She just

2

couldn't give him the satisfaction, as much as her tongue vibrated with a good telling off.

Ernie dumped the bag on the floor, giving a suspicious sniff as he watched Lupin retreat into the corner to busy herself with some pamphlets.

Over the top of Ernie's dusty old head Janet clocked Tristan striding across the road, satchel banging against his bony hip. On spotting Ernie he swiftly ducked into the bakery next door. She chuckled and prayed that after a lucky escape like that he'd have the decency to fetch in something tasty.

"Got you some fancy cakes for your staff meeting," Ernie panted. "You don't deserve 'em but better in your gob than in landfill, eh?"

For a stranger to hygiene Ernie was oddly particular about the environment.

Janet advanced towards him and gingerly accepted the gift, fingertips nipping the bag. A quick glimpse of the contents revealed dented and unopened boxes of French Fancies, only slightly out of date.

"They're own brand but they've been made in the Mr. Kipling factory," he explained, making his way to the newspapers, pulling up his suit trousers as he went. "You can keep the bag."

The bag was in ribbons but Janet accepted it graciously and left Ernie to his obituaries.

The day was mild, the library was boiling hot and Janet could already feel a rivulet of sweat pool in the small of her back. She slipped her hand into her trouser pocket (navy blue chinos with a knife-sharp crease), pulled out her lipstick and armed her pout with a slick of cherry red *Midnight Tease*. She watched the rest of her team arrive, enjoying the moment before the news.

———————— *** ————————

"Pete, love, you can tell the time, can't you?"

Janet made a show of bringing her second-best dress watch, (Thursday market purchase, no regrets), up to her ear and shaking it.

The young man shuffled into the kitchen with his head down and made straight for the kettle. He filled it with cold water and switched it on, hoping against hope that a lovely fresh cuppa would disguise and forgive his very real lack of timekeeping and general social skills.

"Sorry, Janet."

Janet watched Pete carefully rinse and dry four mugs. He was an awkward lad and if he ever entered a tea-making competition he might well win a special mention. Every Council department had to have an apprentice, and it could be worse; Waste Management was stuck with a seventeen year-old germaphobe who couldn't look at a picture of a bag of rubbish without dry heaving.

"Come on, lad, make us our tea and then take a pew," she said. "We've lots to get through."

***

The group huddled together on four stackable chairs in the tiny kitchen, elbows and knees competing for space with book trolleys and recycling bins.

Lupin clutched her notebook and sparkling pink pen; it was her turn to take the minutes. She sensed a dark cloud settling over the group. Janet's aura in particular was in need of a good wash; it was murky and sad.

"Right folks, let's get started," Janet instructed, patting her hair.

The kitchen door shook with a thunderous crash. Pete squeaked and tipped forward.

"Bloody hell!" growled Tristan, as Pete's tea embraced his lap with a sopping wet kiss.

"Oh calm down, Tristan, it's mostly milk," Janet laughed, reaching from her seat to pull open the door.

"You're here, thank God," said a large blue head, followed by a body a kind person might have described as 'privileged'.

Lupin closed her eyes and started to visualise a wide, open space. Green field, blue sky. A cow or

5

two. Maybe some wildflowers for a pop of colour. An oxygen tank.

"Hello, Violet, what can we do you for?" asked Janet, knowing full well that a Monday morning without a disruption wasn't a Monday morning at all.

Violet of the indigo hair wedged herself between Pete and Tristan and stumbled into the centre of the circle. Pete recoiled. Tristan was still mopping the tea from his jeans.

All four casually edged their chairs as far back as they would go.

"Helen is here and she did NOT book in," Violet announced to the room, breathless and wide-eyed.

No-one spoke.

The woman rolled her eyes so far back into her head it looked painful. "I haven't a pattern for her, Janet," she snapped, swaying on her block heels. "Any wonder I'm in bad fettle."

Janet clocked that Violet was wielding a rather large knitting needle. Like a knife.

"You know we have a mostly working photocopier, Violet. Run her off a copy and you'll come out of this the bigger woman."

Tristan's face was a picture.

"I suppose I could," she conceded. "Black and white, mind. Any more colour copies and the cake kitty'll dry up and then Tina will never come back. It's a balancing act, Janet. You'll know what I'm talking about."

Violet plopped a hand on Pete's head and levered herself out of the circle. His eyes welled with tears.

"Why can't she just pop her head in and say hello, like a normal person?" Lupin asked, watching Violet carefully slam the door behind her.

Janet shook her head. She'd lose her nerve if they didn't get a move on.

"Vi's Vi, Lup. She needs a morning drama like your crystals need a new moon. Now, let's get on before Ernie makes off with the newspapers again."

All eyes were on her. Lupin's pen hovered over a fresh page.

"I've had word from my source at the office of The Powers That Be," Janet began. "We're at serious risk."

Tristan crossed his arms and calmly observed Janet. "At risk of what?"

"Closure, Tristan."

Chapter Two

The number 68 skidded to a stop and discharged Courtney by the multi-storey car park, a grey-fronted affair that overlooked the harbour.

She tripped along the pavement, watching early morning bargain hunters swarm across the sun-streaked shopping precinct, clutching their bags for life. Pulling an elastic from her pocket, she gathered her damp brown hair and whipped it into a messy bun.

In her old school bag she'd squeezed her learning folder, two cling-filmed corned beef sandwiches slathered in brown sauce, five warm cans of Red Bull, a blue pen, and a bulging makeup bag.

Shivering in her crop top and skinnies she wished she'd thrown on her fleece. She'd gotten it free from one of those job fairs she was forced to attend every few months. It was bright yellow, had 'Tynedale Animal Feed' splashed all over it and it came with a key ring and the exhibitor's phone number. That happened to Courtney a lot.

She popped her head into 'The La'al Teacake' for a crack and whiff of fresh bread.

"Alright, our Courtney?" A tall, strongly-built woman with a cap of bright red hair stood with her back to the counter, tidying a stack of plum breads.

"How'd you know it was me, Eileen?" Courtney asked, hand on hip.

"'Cos I can smell that nasty perfume you take a bath in. It's rank." Eileen turned to her and laughed. "Aw now, a certain young lad will love it. That's the main thing, eh?"

"Dunno what you're talking about," Courtney snapped. "Anyway, I need half a dozen custard tarts. Please."

Eileen shook her head. "Too late, chick, Tristan's been in and bought them. I think he was trying to avoid Ernie."

"Has that old scrote been in already?" Courtney briefly considered getting back on the bus and into her warm bed.

"Came in special, just to show off his bin cakes. Then he had the cheek to ask for yesterday's bread when I'd already given him some last night."

"Well, did you give it to him?" Courtney's stomach rumbled. She'd missed breakfast and had a good mind to dig out a corned beef sandwich, but eating processed meat at ten in the morning just seemed wrong. *Maybe I'll have it in the loo.*

"Yeah, 'course I did. It was only a few cheese scones and a sliced white. Bless him."

***

9

Courtney slipped in through the side entrance, (she had history with the revolving door), and dashed across the floor, narrowly avoiding Ernie who was ripping articles out of the Seatown Chronicle with cheese scone-encrusted fingers.

Ducking between Romance and Horror she reached the public loo, free to scoff her sandwich without judgement. An acrid blend of stale poo, Febreze and Janet's hand cream hit her upon entering the cramped room, but she soldiered on.

Door locked, Courtney shook her bag from her shoulders and pulled out the sad excuse for a snack. In a bizarre food experiment, the bread, beef, sauce and cling film had fused into what looked like a ball of mixed plasticine.

"I need a lunch box."

She turned to toss it in the bin. "BLOODY HELL! Ernie, you dirty bugger!"

Out of the corner of her eye Courtney had spotted the tell-tale yellow dribble of a sink-polluter.

She gathered her things and abandoned the scene of the crime.

The scrawny man shuddered in his seat as Courtney whirled past the doorway, eyes blazing.

He had the computer suite to himself, all one hundred and forty four square feet of it. On a good day, four out of the five computers worked. The printer was a sentient being that doled out ink on paper as regularly as Ernie spent actual money.

Hunched over Computer 3, (his computer), Stan Tweddle struggled to contain his rage. Firstly, the Madeleine Pit Library business centre was simply not private enough for his crucial clandestine concerns and secondly, hussies like Courtney Harrison had no place in a public facility funded by responsible citizens.

Sighing, he adjusted his seat and continued with his project. The dark loading screen reflected a deeply dissatisfied face. Full red cheeks surrounded a pointed, imperious nose. His thin, pale lips were besieged by tiny furrows, the result of decades of disapproval. Thick salt and pepper hair stood upright and proud. All in all, a solid man with concrete, immovable beliefs.

A tall woman sporting a bright yellow tracksuit strode through the doorway. "Well then, Mr Tweddle," she bellowed. "Who's on your list today? Mind if I join you? I'm Skyping my new toy boy in Singapore."

Stan was resolute in his hatred for Bev Rogers. She always knew when he was in the library. Always. A more suspicious man would think his privacy has been compromised.

"I'm not biting, Bev," he shouted at the screen, refusing to look at her. "Toddle on down to Age

Support, they'll hook you up with your granny grabber."

"Alright, soldier, don't get your boxers in a bunch," she laughed, waving a sheet of paper. "I'm only putting up a poster for the fancy dress 5k."

Bev chuckled her way out of the room leaving Stan once again with his letter of concern.

Stan Tweddle had been on the television many times. When the regional news station needed a bit of local colour to comment on anything from foot and mouth to controversial pizza toppings, they wheeled him out. He only had two demands: that they film him in front of the Seatown harbour memorial and 'thank' him in fish and chips (but only from the Saveloy Savoy, never from Marconi's).

The day Stan discovered the blind carbon copy function on his AOL email account was a momentous one. The hours, nay days, spent emailing editors one at a time were a distant memory.

Staring resolutely at his computer he continued his painfully slow one-fingered typing.

The world turned, paint dried and Janet reapplied her lipstick six times.

Satisfied, he pressed send.

This is going to blow the whole rotten system wide open.

***

"Closing? Who, us?" asked Lupin, her heartbeat quickening from a gentle canter to an *'Oh holy God, where does this bleedin' horse think it's going?'* gallop. She wasn't sure what to write on her fresh page. The sparkly pen was desperate to make contact with the paper but Lupin's sensitive nature flatly refused to scribe such emotionally painful words.

"Yes. Maybe. Probably," Janet sighed, picking fluff from her pink cardigan. "I'm sorry folks, but according to them up high our numbers are falling and the Council can't justify continuing the operation in its present form."

Tristan sat up. "The *operation*?" he spat. "Bloody fascists. What happened to educating the great unwashed? Afraid the free WiFi will spark a revolution?"

Janet looked around the clean, tired room. It took pennies to keep the place going; the last time it had undergone a refit was in preparation for a royal visit. From Princess Di. This threat wasn't about footfall.

Tristan had read her mind. "It's premium land, Jan. Ripe for a big development. I'm telling you, two years from now we'll be sitting in yet another bloody Gregg's."

"What's wrong with Gregg's?" piped up Pete. He could only eat beige; Gregg's was his lifeline.

Tristan shook his head and scowled at Pete. "Of course, what was I thinking!" he snapped, throwing his hands in the air. "Who needs the key to knowledge, for free no less, when we've got yet another Gregg's spewing out manky sausage rolls and caramel custard doughnuts!"

"Sorry, Tristan." Pete shrunk into his baggy old school shirt. Lupin gave him a friendly wink and pondered how on earth a lad so smitten with sausage rolls could be that thin. *A young man's metabolism is a miraculous thing.*

She turned on Tristan. "Tristan, this isn't about greasy pastry. Apologise to poor Pete."

"Sorry, young Pete. It's just so bloody unfair." Tristan put his head in his hands, gripping his shaggy fair hair with clenched fingers. He stared at the floor, noticing not for the first time that Maeve the cleaner still hadn't managed to scrape off the red glitter Vi had 'accidentally' spilled after a fight over who had stolen her craft club milk (Janet). *That stuff will be there till the end of time; Gregg's or no Gregg's.*

Pete sat up and smiled. "Should I put the kettle on?" His last cup had ended up on Tristan's trousers, after all.

Janet couldn't help but grin. *That indomitable British spirit buggering up my big announcement.* "Yes lad, put the kettle on and Tristan can get his tarts out. I'm meeting Amanda soon and I'll get to the bottom of this, I promise."

***

14

The woman snaked her hand around a mountain of angora wool and delicately snagged another digestive biscuit. She was slight of build and simmered with energy, something Violet couldn't countenance. *Sitting there in her ecru tunic and big necklace, eating my biscuits.*

"So anyway, Vi, I've heard you're thinking of starting a creative writing club?" the munching woman asked, spitting crumbs all over her warm from the copier knitting pattern, (ribbon-laced baby bootees).

"Oh, did you now, Helen," Violet replied, tilting her head back to make eye contact with the others around the trestle table. "Where did you hear that?"

Malcolm looked guilty, clicking and clacking his number seven needles, wishing he could melt into a puddle on the library floor. Helen had the decency not to meet her confidant's eyes. "Just whispers, Vi, you know how it is." She resumed casting on the lemon angora wool. "Is it a private club then? Because I've been published."

Violet bristled and busied herself with swiping biscuit crumbs onto the floor. "Really, Helen? Tell us more about this epic bestseller that seems to have bypassed the library shelves."

Tina sat at the top of the table, parked next to a modest 'Seatown Tourism' stand that consisted of a clutch of leaflets advertising fishing boat trips and a chocolate making workshop. There was also a lone, torn leaflet for the long since closed Madeleine Pit Mining Museum. She tittered into her lukewarm tea.

Helen swung her necklace in Tina's direction. "I have been published! I came fourth in a short story competition held by this very library."

"Really dear?" Violet asked innocently. "It's just that you've never mentioned it before."

'Oh, bugger off, Vi," Helen sulked. "You're just jealous. But I'm over it, so can I join your club? I might be able to help, you know, with hints and tips and stuff."

Violet considered the craft group her family. She knew their little foibles; every dropped stitch was *her* dropped stitch. She loved them, but they were a right pain in the backside.

The tinny clang of dropped needles made Violet look up. Malcolm was standing with his back to her, peering over the 'Falls Prevention Week - Get Your Free Slippers' display. "Drama!" he whispered, adjusting his tortoiseshell glasses.

Collectively, the crafters leaned back on their chairs.

They watched as Lupin marched out of the kitchen, gripping her sparkly pen, fluffy purple handbag swinging from her shoulder.

"Lupin has some lovely clothes, doesn't she?" Malcolm remarked, still gaping as she left the building at speed.

_____ *** _____

"What's up with Lup?" Tristan asked as he stalked the kitchen, which took all of four seconds.

"I dunno, Tristan," Janet replied, staring up at him as he attempted to stretch his legs. "I shouldn't think she'd be too worried about her job, considering she came here on secondment six years ago. She can just go back to Finance."

Pete eyed the kettle. His interlaced fingers itched for the touch of cold steel. *Maybe I could get a job in Gregg's. Making teas and bacon butties might be alright. I'd have to learn all about coffee though.*

Janet watched Pete's face scrunch up in thought. *He's probably wondering if Gregg's are recruiting.* "Don't worry our Peter, these things take forever to work themselves out. You'll be safe for a while yet." She leaned over and gave him a gentle pat on the shoulder.

Tristan dropped back into his chair. "Yeah, but Lup is the chilled one, Janet. Doesn't bode well."

"She's become very attached to the place, Tristan. Finance has asked her back more than once, you know. Not that I should be telling you that. But she's always managed to convince them to let her stay here."

"For all of her weirdness, she is a good manager," Tristan conceded, before slapping his knees and turning to Pete. "Come on then, lad, what's keeping you?"

Pete jumped up and took some clean cups down from the cupboard.

Chapter Three

After work...

Janet decided to leave her car at the Mad Pit and walk the short distance home.

Strolling along a windy High Street she watched energetic mothers bounce grizzling toddlers from pound shop to pound shop and old gents smoke and sip coffee outside a rammed Costa Coffee.

Janet closed her eyes as she passed the off licence. *A nice bottle of crisp, cold sauv blanc is exactly not what I need right now,* she thought, fiddling with the lipstick in her pocket. *What I need is a miracle. And a big bag of Maltesers.*

"Y'alright, love?" asked a lady in a crimson head scarf, after watching Janet blindly walk into a post box.

Janet rubbed her arm, feeling a combination of absolute mortification and a desperate thirst for fermented grape juice. She looked at the woman in her smart wool coat with matching head gear. *Looks like Mrs Claus is having a well deserved day off. Good on her.*

"Oh, aye, I'm fine. Thanks for asking." She winced as pain bloomed in her upper arm.

Looking Janet up and down, the woman adjusted her scarf. "You work in the library, don't you, lass?"

Janet nodded. "Do you pop in, yourself?"

"From time to time, just to check on things," the woman replied with a smile.

Very enigmatic for Santa's missus. "Well, things could be better but I just work there. Anyway, sorry to trouble you and thanks for making sure I hadn't brained myself," Janet joked as she started to back away.

"That library is the backbone of this town, and we need it now more than ever," the woman lamented, looking around and shaking her head.

Janet stopped and squinted past her new friend. A gaggle of young people were exiting the pub and judging by the state of them they'd been there since opening.

The girls were clad in the same uniform of tight black jeans, white trainers and furry-hooded coats, the lads decked out in sports tops and tracksuit bottoms.

"I couldn't agree more but unfortunately I've got no control over that. A few months from now you might see me falling out of there," she joked, pointing to the gang of drinkers.

"Well, we'll see about that," the woman in red said, walking away. "Good luck, lass."

Janet shivered, then turned and continued on her way.

***

Later that night...

"Will you please shut up back there!" remonstrated the bearded man, his hulking figure swaddled in a thick cream fisherman's sweater. Beads of sweat christened his upper lip, fighting for space with the foam of a locally brewed deep, golden ale. One hairy hand gripped a mic, the other his pint; he was damned if the Tequila Mockingbirds were going to ruin another pub quiz.

The trio of women adorned in their midweek best giggled around a pitcher of mojito.

"Just admit you can't handle us winning, Alan!" teased the ringleader, a thirty-something brunette in thick tortoiseshell glasses.

Tristan shook his head and silently urged Alan to move on to the history round. He was sick of these weekly shenanigans with the Birds. Alan clearly fancied Denise but he was too stupid, sweaty and hairy to do anything about it.

"For the sake of my sanity let's all break for ten minutes," Alan bellowed. "Next up is the history round. Keep your answer sheets safe and no looking on your mobile phones in the loos." He made a point of glowering at Tequila Mockingbirds but they'd already scarpered to the Ladies.

"It's your round, mate," said the thin, black haired man sitting opposite Tristan. He was decked out in a spotless navy blue checked shirt and stiff, freshly washed black jeans.

His special pub quiz pen, (a thirty-eighth birthday gift from his girlfriend), nestled on his special pub quiz notebook, (a thirty-eighth birthday gift from his mum).

Tristan stood up and stretched, his fingers grazing the crumbling ceiling of the 'Drunken Sailor' inn. Something soft and delicate clung to them and he rubbed his hands in disgust. *Bloody spiders.*

"It might be my last round for a bit, marra," he replied with a lopsided grin, looking down at Dean. "Looks like the Mad Pit is going to close."

"That's bad luck that, Tristan. I'll have another pint of bitter."

And that was that.

_____ *** _____

At around the same time...

Pete pretended the ball hadn't hit him in the face and resumed taking attendance.

Inwardly, he conceded that doing this little job was easier when twenty-six kids weren't running around a small church hall like they had rockets up their arses. Indeed, if he'd been organised and not in the kitchen making tea for himself and the other volunteers, he could have ticked each demon child off the list as it had erupted into the building.

The offending tween returned his attention to the ball and booted it onto a wobbly craft table sending loo rolls, glitter glue and safety scissors crashing into the laps of squealing girls.

"Josh Two, please don't do that," Pete pleaded, but his voice barely carried above the riot of noise. *I need a big whistle. And one of those tablets mam hides in her handbag.*

"Pete, your girlfriend's here!" cried a large group of twelve year old girls. Too old for team games but too young to sneak out for a shifty smoke they spent their nights gleefully torturing Pete in St. John's hall.

He turned on his heel to see Courtney skulking at the hall door. Children zipped past her at warp speed, a blur of primary colours and spit.

"Alright, Courtney?" he asked, tripping over a lone hula hoop on his way to where she stood. "You here to pick up Nathan?"

"He's not here, he's grounded for nicking nana's bingo winnings again." She kicked the toe of her boot against the skirting board. Ten year-old Nathan was so notoriously light-fingered his mother had been reduced to sewing up his pockets.

"Oh, I never noticed." Pete needed to seriously review the attendance protocol. He could have sworn he'd seen Nathan scoping out the tuck shop earlier. All ten-year olds looked the same to him.

Courtney stroked her long hair and moved closer. As the sting of her perfume hit the back of Pete's throat he choked, tried to hold in the cough and failed, dousing her in spittle.

"Pete!" She jumped back and tripped over two youngsters engaged in a wrestling match.

"Sorry, Courtney, I had something in my throat," Pete squeaked. "Lads, can you please do whatever that is on the gym mat?" The sweaty pair yelped and tore up the hall like feral pups.

"Did you know Ernie peed in the sink this morning?" she asked, curling a lock of hair around her finger. In the far reaches of her mind she knew the vagaries of flirting were lost on Pete. "He's disgusting! Why do you let him in the library?'"

Pete pulled a face. "Gross. I'll tell Janet he's been at it again. Anyway, he'll have to use his own loo soon enough."

"What do you mean?"

"Well," he whispered, "the library's probably going to close in a few months. Crap, eh?"

"You're lying, right?" Courtney looked close to tears. So did Pete. He was useless around weeping women.

"Apparently not enough people are using it? Council expects hundreds to come in and that."

Pete considered his position for a second. The youth club had offered to pay him to work a few hours a week but he'd rather watch Ernie abuse the library toilet than get sucked into that vortex of pain. Volunteering suited him, he could walk away any time he wanted. In actual fact Pete couldn't walk away when it suited him because his mother had committed him to helping out. This was because he had graffitied 'I hate Pernod' on the church bench on a drunken dare.

Courtney had her own thoughts on the matter. *The Job Centre will send me to Southbridge Training and I can't handle that Maisie one..she hates me...she always keeps the window open and the biscuits are stale.*

——————— *** ———————

A little later...

Lupin sat cross-legged on the living room floor, black cat snoring on one side of her, a glass of wine and smouldering cigarette on the other. In front of her was a paperback copy of the book of the month: 'The Time Traveller's Wife'.

After storming out of work Lupin had gone straight home, changed into her softest, comfiest clothes and meditated like her life had depended on it. She had lit sandalwood incense sticks on any surface that wasn't covered in crystals, books and candles. She'd also attempted some light astral projection and was peacefully cruising the rings of Saturn when Freya chose to nip her on the toes with tiny sharp teeth.

Lupin was in a terrible quandary. Worlds were colliding. Great yawning chasms were threatening to swallow her whole. But first she had to top-up the prosecco-flavoured kettle crisps.

"It just really confused me, you know? I couldn't keep up with all the zipping between timelines." This was from her book club bestie, Alison. Alison came for the wine, the snacks, and the chat.

"I found their relationship incredibly destructive, one-sided and inappropriate. Especially when Claire was a child." This was Kate. She read every book, every month and took the book club *very* seriously.

"Yes, it was icky, Kate. Now, where have you stashed that wine, Lupin?" This was Lizzy. She was in a complicated relationship and came to share all of her problems.

"It's on the worktop, behind you, Liz." Lizzy turned from her warm seat in the living room and reached out to grab the sweating chardonnay from the kitchen.

Lupin remained in the lotus position as her friends lounged on the squashy orange sofa. The sole reason for this lack of space was not because Lupin actually enjoyed sitting on her bones. And the girls were great chums who didn't mind sharing what was for all intents and purposes an oversized armchair so big it blocked out every inch of natural light in her tiny flat.

There would be little rest for Lupin tonight. After dissecting Lizzy's love life her friends would go on their way, she'd clean up and then she'd mull over her rapidly diminishing options until the sun rose over the horizon and Freya cried for food.

***

At the same time...

The woman with the bright blonde hair scaled the groaning ladder and pulled herself into the attic. Pulling on a light chord she squinted into the dank, neglected space. What little light there was was dim and filled with dancing dust. She ignored the scurrying of little feet and moved forward on her knees.

Her eyes landed on the box.

Should have brought my duster with me, this place is filthy.

Chapter Four

Amanda spun around in her swivel chair. Then spun some more. The Community Services Manager grabbed her cup of coffee and had another go. This time with her eyes closed. As she slowed a splotch of warm coffee spilled onto her second best suit trousers, (Next's Boxing Day sale; her mother had queued from 5am). She placed the cup on her desk, pulled a tissue from her cube of luxury soft tissues, (Monet's Water Lilies print), and dabbed at the spreading stain on her lap. *I'll not try that again.*

"Hello? Amanda?" The squeak barely travelled between the open-plan office and her cheap plywood door. A faint knock-knock followed.

Bloody hell. "Come in, Barry."

The door opened and a curly brown head popped through followed by a trim body clad in smart/casual office chic; shades of grey that blended perfectly with the brutalist second-floor decor.

"Morning, Amanda!" Barry piped, looking around her office. "Oops, you've spilled your coffee!"

Amanda looked him in the eye. "Yes, Barry, I have spilled my coffee. Why are you here?"

Barry shifted from foot to foot. "Well, Janet's here, isn't she?"

Oh God. She opened her A4 Seatown Council desk diary and flicked through it. There, written in green ink with a hugely messy asterisk by it read: 'Janet, POSSIBLE LIBRARY CLOSURE meeting 10am'.

Out of the corner of her eye Amanda glanced at her favourite poster (one of four on her cork board). Large white letters on a mountainous background, rock climber clinging to the edge of a deadly cliff: 'When the going gets tough, the tough get going'. But it didn't help. She wasn't tough, she wanted to go far, far away from Janet and that day centre for weirdos.

"Okay, Baz, let her in," she sighed. "Oh, and ask her if she wants a hot drink. And get me another coffee. And some plain biscuits. Please!"

Amanda pulled a fresh notebook from her drawer stash. Before closing the drawer, she grabbed a hairbrush and smoothed down her brazilian blow dry.

Now she was ready.

———————— *** ————————

"Amanda."

"Janet."

"Ladies! Sit down and enjoy your coffee and *biz*quits. Amanda, just shout if you need anything."

Barry left the two women to their staring contest and returned to his Odin's Berserkers Reenactment online group chat.

Amanda swung on her chair a little before stopping herself. "It's been a while since you were here, Janet. Do you think it's changed much?"

"Not really, 'Mand." Janet listened to the ear-splitting cattle market that lay on the other side of the door. Dozens of overworked, committed people failing to please falsely confident, incompetent middle managers.

"Really? We've got a vending machine now. There's fruit in it."

Janet offered a fake, approving nod.

Amanda opened her notebook and smoothed down the first virgin page. So satisfying. Everything she wrote down would be typed up by Barry, post-meeting and saved in her departmental drive, then entered once more, word for word, into the internal recording system, then copied and pasted into a document and saved in a management team folder entitled, 'Madeleine Pit Library'.

"So, Janet. The reason we're here. The Mad Pit is getting ever closer to shutting, I'm afraid."

Janet crossed her legs and leaned forward. Amanda leaned back.

"Uh-huh. Why isn't Barry taking the minutes?" Janet asked, clasped hands hugging her knees.

"Well, I thought it would be nice for us to have a little chat first, before we go 'official.'" She actually made air quotes.

Janet thought this was absolutely hilarious and demonstrated her merriment by quietly clearing her throat.

This terrified Amanda. And she was certain Janet's hair had gotten bigger.

"Gotcha, you don't want me to embarrass you in front of Barry. Fair enough, lass. Let's get on," Janet said, sitting back on her too-small plastic chair, (a classic Amanda Power Move). "I know the Pit is standing in the way of your budget cuts, so let's not pretend that you care about keeping us open."

Amanda had the decency to blush. "Yes, let's move on, Jan. We've been reviewing the situation for over a year now and we just can't justify the numbers. Between you and me, Seatown is being forced to sell off a number of properties just to pay the bills."

"So, what are we saying here then? How long have we got and what's the exit plan?" Janet pulled out her own notebook, a soft, faded effort that had been witness to a lot of action.

"Exit plan?" Amanda wrote down 'exit plan'. Then added a question mark.

"Yes, what happens to our users if we close. Where would they go? And how will our resources be distributed?"

"Well, you'd all be moved into other positions within the Council. And we're considering a mobile library service. But nothing's been decided yet."

Janet pulled out her lipstick. Amanda held her breath.

"Mobile library service, eh?" On went a slick of *Devil Woman*. "Not much room for an IT class in a mobile van, is there?"

Amanda exhaled just as her vision had started to darken. *Where are you, Baz, when I need you to pester me?*

"As you know, Janet, there are community centres that already deliver training courses that your users can access."

Janet held up her hand. "I'll stop you there, Amanda. Firstly, these classes are only for unemployed young people and secondly, they're not on the bus route for the vast majority of members that live in the town centre."

"There's Age Support, don't forget."

"Yes, they're doing a sterling job, 'Mand but you and I both know that their contract isn't going to be renewed."

"That's a headache for another meeting," Amanda sighed, pulling on her shiny, chestnut locks. She met Janet's eyes. "We can't give the library much more time, Jan. We're desperate for funds and a decision will be made soon."

"I don't buy it," Janet whispered, leaning towards the Community Services Manager. "You're sounding a bit creaky, Amanda. I think your corporate robot suit needs oiling."

———————— *** ————————

Taking the lift was not an option, Janet needed to move at speed.

She flew down the stairs, barely waiting for the automatic door to wake up before exiting into the packed car park. Gathering herself, she pulled out her phone and texted Tristan: *We're closing. We're done.*

She heard the ping halfway to her car.

We're not and we're not.

Chapter Five

Violet woke up grinning.

Her dreams had been awash with success. She'd been awash with John's sweat too, as he was a hairy chap with hot blood, but mostly she had been doing the backstroke in a sea of thrilling fame.

In one exceptionally satisfying dreamlet she had been in the Mad Pit, sat on an emerald-studded golden throne, signing her Sunday Times bestseller for hundreds of fans; every one of whom looked exactly like Helen, down to the abstract jewellry and oat-coloured capsule wardrobe. The line of Helens snaked around the library and all the way down to the multi-storey car park.

Putting on her glasses she picked up the sheet of paper that rested on her bedside table. A mess of scribbles met her bleary eyes:

Old Italian disc jockey
Tall woman in tortoiseshell glasses
Seatown swimming champion with a shiny scalp
Chasing sheep in the ballroom

Her nocturnal scrawls made little sense but with a bit of effort she was confident she could scrape together an intriguing short story. *Or maybe a novella.*

Slowly, she eased herself up from bed and opened the curtains. Beyond her tidy front garden lay the sparkling Irish sea, and somewhere deep in Seatown, John was walking their Cavoodle, Agatha C.

Today was the inaugural meeting of the creative writing club and Violet had pencils to sharpen.

_____ *** _____

Courtney woke up in a panic.

She couldn't believe that she'd overslept, today of all days.

Now her mum had slipped into the bathroom to slap on cheap foundation and wail to Michael Bublé on the shower radio.

Her nana would be needing a wash soon, too.

Snuggled under her thick duvet she gave herself one more minute before she was forced to drag her mother out by the extensions.

_____ *** _____

Pete was roused from a fitful sleep by the reassuring, floral aroma of brewing Earl Grey.

The Teasmade had been a gift from his mother, a tea connoisseur with the most exquisite taste. Pete had attempted many times to acquire his mum's discerning palate but discovered early on that his limit was a morning Earl Grey with lemon. After that, it was builder's tea all the way.

———————— *** ————————

Ernie had forgotten to go to sleep.

———————— *** ————————

Maeve was elbow-deep in suds when dawn broke outside the 'Drunken Sailor' pub.

Pint glasses teeming with rainbow bubbles clinked in the old Belfast sink. Hundreds of mementos and artefacts crowded cobwebbed, rotten shelves. The trinkets were never dusted for fear of liberating the cantankerous spirits of spiteful seamen; or so Maeve had led everyone to believe.

She loved the creepy old pub; having it to herself was so electrifying her flesh would shiver into goosebumps.

But today Maeve had to leave early.

She had another errand to run and the timing had to be right.

———————— *** ————————

Spark Pug dreamed he was laying waste to a bowlful of liver-flavoured candy floss.

Janet awoke to a dog licking her hairline and breathing into her ear.

The pungent scent of puppy breath forced her out of bed and into the day.

 ***

Last night Tristan had joyfully discovered that five pints were sufficiently capable of making him forget his impending redeployment to Parking Enforcement.

This morning he remembered that the previous night had been a school night.

 ***

Lupin's laptop bathed her bedroom in a soft, blue light. Had it not been the witching hour and the glow highlighting mega powerful online anti-anxiety spells, it might have been cosy.

Lupin was in knots, inside and out, (lotus position, smoky quartz crystal in her pyjama bottom pocket and unresolved Irritable Bowel Syndrome).

Every nerve was on high alert despite the seventeen flickering green candles and cinnamon incense.

Lying spices. Lying candles.

Chill out, Lup.

"They call me Mellow Yellow...quite rightly."
Bugger, should I have been burning yellow candles?

She flopped back onto her bed.

The dreams were getting worse. Each hellish fragment threw up a riot of colour, chaos and devilment. In this nightmarish universe everything could be bought for a price and the air was heavy with the tang of salt.

_____ *** _____

There was a queue outside the library that morning.

At the head of it was Violet, armed for instant stardom bearing an immaculate copy of the 'Writers' and Artists' Yearbook'.

Courtney raced past 'The La'al Teacake' but stood far enough behind Violet so as not to encourage conversation.

Ernie stumbled up bearing gifts, his vessel of choice a wet cardboard box containing a moth-eaten bin bag of stale Viennese Whirls and a stack of damp paper.

He seemed unduly excited with his haul and nudged Courtney with a bony elbow. "Alright, lass?"

Courtney turned to face the erstwhile sink fouler. "Hiya, Ernie. What've you got there?"

"Well now," he declared proudly, juggling his wares. "I've got you all some Morrison's cakes."

"From the bin?"

"Aye, love. It's Morrison's day, eh? And I found this box of old stuff beside them so reckoned it might keep that mardy arse, Twistam, happy for a week or two."

Courtney reckoned it would go straight into the recycling bin.

_____ *** _____

Janet rounded the corner to three vibrating people. They made her feel itchy. And a bit panicked.

Good Cumbrian manners prevented the trio from rushing Janet; instead they did a kind of hokey cokey jig; one leg in, one leg out and lots of shaking about. Ernie's crooked rumba was dynamite.

She sighed and opened the library door.

_____ *** _____

"Janet, Janet, Janet!" Courtney's tightly-knotted ponytail had weaponised, forcing Janet to duck as it advanced towards its target.

"Courtney, love, I've had enough hair mares this morning and I don't need an eye taking out by that helicopter blade of yours," Janet warned, backing away from the entrance. "Can you calm down?"

"Sorry, Jan, it's just...I know. You know?" Courtney's bottom lip trembled as she slumped down onto a kid's beanbag.

Janet knew. *Pete and his big gob.*

"Can you just keep it to yourself for the time being, Court? We've got to think about our next steps and I don't need Violet blaming it on my shade of lipstick or Lupin's insistence on cleansing the library with sage every full moon. Alright?"

Courtney nodded. She pulled out a Red Bull and popped it open, careful not to spill any on the Beatrix Potters.

"It doesn't mean you can drink that rubbish though, young lady. We're not closed yet!"

Janet turned on her kitten heel and marched into the staff room before anyone else could accost her.

***

Ernie tumbled through the library doors like a poor man's Norman Wisdom, his crumbling box spewing its mouldy contents onto the floor.

As he was on his hands and knees gathering up paper and pastry, a lanky pair of denim-clad legs side-stepped him at speed.

"Tristram, just the lad!"

Tristan gathered up all of the goodwill his hangover could muster and turned to the prostrate man. "What have you got there, Ernie? Your memoirs?"

Ernie took a minute to straighten himself and corral his pride. He shook down his best tweed jacket and wiped wet paper from his jogging bottoms.

"For your information, Mr. Local History, I came upon this rare and significant find during my morning walk and thought it might be of interest to your crusty old brain."

"Who are you calling old, Methuselah? And exactly how close to Morrison's *was* this stuff?" Tristan hunkered down for a healthy sniff of the documents. They smelt like student kitchen cupboards.

"Close enough, smart arse," Ernie lied. "Tek it or leave it. But if you leave it, you can dispose of it. And not in the general rubbish."

Tristan swept the stack of paper into his arms with a view to giving it a swift burial in a dark corner of the kitchen.

Ernie settled himself into his favourite orange pleather armchair. "And don't forget the cakes! They're Janet's favourites. Sweet and crumbly, just like her."

***

Earlier that morning.

"John, love, can you pass me my briefcase?"

Violet sat on the Chesterfield, squeezing her feet into black patent court shoes, (with a two inch heel); not too dressy but smart enough to show authority. She hated her morning feet; they were swollen and obnoxious, desperate to remain cocooned inside their fuschia pink fake-Ugg slippers.

John toddled into the living room, briefcase in hand. "Right-oh, love. Are you ready?"

"Lemme just check I've got everything I need before we set off."

Violet gently placed her brown leather briefcase onto the floor and pinged it open. Nestled inside were three fluffy pencil cases stuffed with multi-coloured biros, a selection of crease-free notebooks in bright primary shades and a dictaphone for when inspiration struck. There was no room for the 'Writers' and Artists' Yearbook' which, of course, Violet found immensely satisfying. *Oh well, I'll just have to carry it.*

She looked up at John, who was twirling his keys. "I'm ready."

Inside the Library.

Violet clicked her fingers.

She's actually *clicking her fingers, the brazen hussy.* Janet slowed her pace, deliberately avoiding eye contact with the woman and her briefcase.

"Janet, darling, I asked for two trestle tables today? We'll need to *spread out.*"

Janet turned on her heel and strode back to the kitchen. "Pete, can you drag out another trestle for the Algonquin Round Table when you're done with your brew?"

Violet had plastered posters the length and breadth of Seatown, at her own cost. She'd lowered herself to beg Courtney to set up a Facebook page. She'd even given a talk to the Seatown U3A, (a golden opportunity to recruit retired teachers), but at ten-thirty who traipsed into the inaugural meeting of the Seatown creative writing club but Tina, Malcolm, and bloody Helen.

"We'll give it another ten minutes, chaps," she said, looking out of the window. Her shoes were pinching. *My muse wants plimsolls.*

"So, uh, what will we be doing today, Vi?" Malcolm inquired, lining up his Derwent HB pencils on the paint-splodged table.

"She'll talk and we'll listen," sniggered Helen.

Malcolm rolled his eyes. "Helen, that's not what I meant; I'm policing pensioner bingo at 12pm and my life won't be worth living if I'm late."

"Let's get a move on, Vi, so we can protect Malcolm's knackers from Elsie's death grip."

"How did you know about Elsie?" Malcolm asked Helen, crossing his legs.

Violet turned from the window and took her seat. "This is NOT the environment for discussing testicles, people. Let's get started."

As Violet passed out her twelve-point agenda, Courtney slithered along the bookshelves and plonked herself down beside Tina and her tray of homemade sweet treats. "Young madam, this is not an accredited course," Violet barked. "Can you please move along?"

Courtney sneered and grabbed a vanilla cupcake, frosting first. *That'll show her.*

"Keep your wig on, Nanna Smurf. I've got something to tell you," she gloated, acutely aware of the sticky sweet frosting coating her fingers. *Gross.*

"We're all ears," Helen said, her eyes flashing. She loved a bit of scandal.

"I'm pretty sure you don't know this," she said with a mouthful of sponge, waving her free hand above her head, "but...this place is closing. This is bloody delicious, Tina, did you make it?"

"I did, our Courtney," Tina said, jubilant. "The secret is an extra egg. Actually,..."

"Will you shut up about cake, Tina!" Violet's face was as pale as the cream frosting. "What do you mean it's closing, Courtney?" She loomed over her, her formidable bust mere inches from the girl's messy bun.

"Pete said last night," she told Violet's mono-boob. "But if ANYONE hears it was me that told you, I'll break every pencil in your briefcase."

Malcolm and Helen were agog. Tina was still glowing from Courtney's praise.

"Why are you all so upset? At least it means Ernie can't piss in the bog sink anymore!"

Violet looked down at the girl. "You'll have to start from the beginning and tell us everything. Leave NOTHING out. You can have another cupcake if you do."

Tina practically slid off her chair in ecstasy.

Chapter Six

Gripping a Debenhams bag, Stan carefully avoided touching anyone as he pounded the mean streets of Seatown.

Inside the plastic bag was enough material to blow the bloated bureaucratic system to smithereens. Stan was very careful not to use incendiary language these days, not since his last warning. But he could do so in his own head; no one could stop him from doing that.

He had painstakingly printed off every email he'd ever received, yet if he knew just how much The Cloud had on him, he'd never get out of the bed in the morning.

As he neared the library he prayed that Bev wouldn't be there. Janet was his target today, not that mouth in a tracksuit.

***

When Stan walked through the library door, he thought there'd been a death. He thought this because Violet was silent. Her acolytes were also hushed. Miss Harrison was laughing and wantonly shoving sponge into her mouth.

"Well, if it t'int 'Betrayed of Seagrove Terrace, Seatown'." Ernie was sitting in his usual spot, licking his way through the dailies.

"What's up with that lot?" Stan asked, standing as far away as he possibly could from Ernie. Stan believed that smells were solid and as such were capable of invading orifices.

"Library's closing, lad." He didn't look up from his page, not wanting to miss anything racy in the obituaries.

"What? Why?" Stan's brain was itchy.

"Dunno, Stan, but my money is on weirdos searching for granny porn on the interweb." Ernie looked up at him and smirked.

This wasn't supposed to happen. "It's imperative that I talk to Janet."

Janet was in her office. Or more accurately, the room she used as an office. In reality it was an upstairs damp overflow space for reserved books and family learning packs. Which happened to have a few chairs, a desk and computer in it. And a big sash window that looked down onto the recycling bins.

She drained her coffee and opened up a spreadsheet. As the page loaded a series of rapid bangs on the door prompted profanities that would make a sailor blush.

"Come in!"

The door swung open and Stan tramped into the room. "Janet. You're not busy, that's good."

"I haven't a care in the world, Stan," she drawled. "Is the printer playing up again?"

"Probably. But that's the least of our worries, lass."

Janet turned to face Stan. "Is this about Bev's posters? Because she's entitled to put them up, Stan."

A ripple of disgust passed over the man's face. "Don't mention that woman's name. Did you know she'd bought herself a foreign boy toy? The web is a stinking pool of depravity and we're all drowning in it."

"But?"

He rolled his eyes. "But that's not why I'm here."

"Take a seat Stan, and tell me what's up,"

He flopped onto the nearest chair. "The library's closing and it's all my fault." He bowed his head, awaiting his punishment.

"You what?"

"I wrote a letter to the papers and now the Council has seen fit to close the Mad Pit. But Janet, my letter didn't get printed. I don't understand? Is there something nefarious going on? Are the paper and the Council in LEAGUE?"

Janet adjusted her specs. It gave her something to do that wasn't laughing.

"Stan Tweddle, what have you done?"

Stan cleared his throat and ran a hand over the batch of large-print Danielle Steele hardbacks that Mrs Butterfield had ordered. The old doll had broken her hip and needed some muscled farm workers to get her through the worst of it. Her daughter was due in later to pick them up; hopefully bearing strong arms and a trolley.

"It's that disgusting Ernie," Stan responded, chin out. "He's the one that's closing the library."

The laugh escaped before she could do anything about it.

Stan stood up and paced the room. "Do you think stale urine in a public facility is funny, Ms Sowerby?" he snarled, grabbing a fluffy duck from the 'Old MacDonald' learning pack.

He started to crush its neck with his long bony fingers.

"What on earth are you on about, Stan?"

"That filthy article empties his bladder in the basin, in a PUBLIC toilet, whenever the fancy takes him! And to add insult to injury, he doesn't even have the courtesy to wash it away!"

"Stan, can you please put the duck down?" Janet's stomach turned. If she'd any hope of keeping the place open she needed to get stuck into the budget, but all she could picture was Ernie relieving himself in the sink.

Stan dropped the duck back into its bag. "Well?"

"Yes, we are aware of this problem," Janet responded. "We've raised it with Mr Noble but he denies it. Maeve does a thorough job of cleaning the loo so I can't imagine you'll have caught anything, Stan."

Stan's cheeks looked hot to the touch. "How can he deny it? I've caught him at it. I was in the cubicle, like a NORMAL person and he hadn't the patience to wait for me to finish! I could HEAR him...tinkling."

"Between you and me he can't hold it in because he has a dodgy prostate. And to be fair to him, if he knows there's a woman in the cubicle he'll go out back," she said, pointing down to the yard. "He knows that we know but that tiny little bit of pride prevents him from admitting it. Because once he does, he'll have to stop."

"So, is Ernie the reason the library's closing?" Stan's expression was a peculiar mix of hope and regret.

"Stan, it's got nowt to do with Ernie's habit, nor was it the result of your letter. Though I would like to put on record that I am thoroughly disappointed in you."

50

Stan was contrite. Which must have hurt.

"Then why are we closing?" he barked. Gloom resumed, ego safely intact.

Janet considered her answer for at least two seconds.

"Because according to the Council, Stan, the library doesn't get used enough."

Stan actually stamped his foot. "Utter codswallop!"

"Unequivocally, Mr Tweddle," Jan smirked.

'Betrayed of Seagrove Terrace' made for the office door. "I'm going to the IT suite, Janet. I may be some time."

***

Lupin dragged the loaded trolley from Science Fiction to Horror, slowly and deliberately restacking books so that they lined up perfectly. Her hands stank of cinnamon and her eyes resembled two lumps of coal. Her weary face bore a faint smile however, because that was her default setting.

Scanning the room she spied a troop of teenage girls huddled around the Young Adult section. Half of them were engaged in serious book hunting, the other half were bent over their phones. She remembered the days of devouring Judy Blume stories and whispering with her girlfriends about periods and first-time sex. She didn't think much had changed since, other than the lingo, and bad perms and pedal pushers had been replaced with carefully curled locks and skinny jeans.

A curly haired girl in black denim approached. "Lupin? Do you know when John Green's new book is coming out?" Her friends giggled, as they always did when any one of them said Lupin's name out loud. It never got old.

Lupin stretched her arms up over her head and yawned dramatically. "In a couple of weeks, Shannon. Do you want us to hold you over a copy?"

"Yeah, that would be great, thanks..em..Lupin."

"No problem. Just go round to the counter with your card and Pete can get it booked in for you."

At the mention of Pete's name any unspoken rule of library civility immediately evaporated and the gang dissolved into ear-splitting giggles. Pete and his floppy hair had that effect.

As Lupin resumed her work she wondered what the Mad Pit would be like without the echo of laughter; when its shelves lay empty and the aroma of dusty paper had long since dissipated.

There *was* one thing she wouldn't miss; Shannon's books coming back reeking of McDonald's chicken nuggets.

_____ *** _____

Over by the counter, Tristan had Pete in a headlock. If truth be told Pete was a bit shocked by the gesture especially since he'd been in the middle of making a room booking with Reverend Nixon, who was now understandably bewildered.

"Listen up, lad," Tristan said. "Before we get into this, make sure you keep your distance from Vi, otherwise she'll snap your arms like mint chocolate Matchsticks."

Pete wriggled free of Tristan's damp armpit and turned his attention back to the vicar. "That's Meeting Room 2 booked for your 'Men's Mental Health Workshop,' Reverend Nixon. Thank you for booking with us again."

The statuesque vicar gripped Pete's hand and gave it a squeeze. "We're never out of the Pit, eh? Thank you sonny, let's hope we get the numbers."

Pete's smile faltered but the vicar didn't notice, his long legs were already halfway home.

Tristan smiled indulgently at his protégé. "Look at you, Peter the Great. Getting very confident, aren't you? You did a good job there."

Pete looked glum. "It hardly matters though, does it?"

Tristan ruffled Pete's hair. "It matters until it doesn't, okay?"

Pete nodded. "So, why do I need protecting from Vi? Should I be scared?"

Tristan rolled up his shirt sleeves. "Very scared."

***

Pete tried to loosen his tie but instead created a knot that would need scissors taking to it at break time. He imagined he and Tristan looked like bouncers at a teenage disco; not exactly threatening but business-like and efficient at sniffing out illicit alcopops.

With his signature professional nonchalance, Tristan loped towards the creative writing club, hands in pockets. Pete rolled up his sleeves, then just as quickly unrolled them; such a brute show of force could prove too much for the ladies. And undermine Malcolm.

Being the unofficial spokesperson of the craft group cum creative writing club, Violet got to her feet and readied herself for war.

Courtney pulled out her third Red Bull of the day and, legs thrumming with caffeine, sat back to enjoy the show.

***

"Ooh, here come the heavies," Violet cackled, brandishing two sharpened pencils at Pete and Tristan. "Do you think we're going to cause a scene?"

Courtney pulled on the hem of Violet's pink cardigan. "Poke 'em with some lead, Vi."

Tristan advanced warily, circling the table of creatives like a wolf.

"Good morning," he said to the blank space above Violet's head. "So, what are you all writing? The Great Cumbrian Novel? Let me guess: two farmers find love at a cattle auction?"

After a great deal of throat clearing, Pete stepped from behind Tristan and attempted to shake a confused Malcolm's hand.

"Malcolm, ladies. You're annoyed because someone told you our news, right?"

Tristan coughed back a laugh.

Courtney spat out the dregs of her energy drink. "I texted you that I'd told them, Pete."

Helen leaned over and removed the drink from Courtney's hands. "That swill will rot your insides, love."

Violet turned on her block heels and aimed a pencil at Helen's sludge coloured wrap top. "Helen, we're not here to talk about the drinking habits of millennials."

"She's Gen Z, actually," retorted Tristan.

Courtney retrieved the empty red bull can and squashed it between her hands. "Okay, boomer."

The delicate veneer of civility was now in pieces and stomped into crumbs on the red carpet-tiled floor. Better behaved library users had started giving serious side-eye. *Surely a library is a haven of peace and quiet contemplation? Why is that lady with the blue hair trying to stab the woman in the cement-coloured top? The weekend certainly starts early in Seatown.*

Everyone was angry.

But not Tina. Tina was topping up the cupcakes.

Pete shuffled over to where she sat. "Are you alright, Tina?"

Tina smiled and shrugged her shoulders. "I suppose I'm not, Pete. The Pit's been my little oasis since Trev died. But what can we do? Have I not borrowed enough books?"

Pete made one of those sympathetic faces he hated. The one where his mouth formed a weird half smile and his eyebrows met his hairline. Like Stan Laurel at a funeral.

Malcolm, who until now had been basking in the drama, patted Tina on the arm. "I think we should fight this. I, for one, can't imagine the library closing and there's no way I'm going to be forced into doing extra shifts at the home. It would be the end of me."

Pete slowly came to the realisation that he was meant for more than tea-making. But as a Council employee, he couldn't be seen supporting the opposition. He would work in the shadows, exchanging information in brown envelopes and using secret Whatsapp groups to organise public meetings and peaceful protests.

"You still with us, Pete?" Tristan asked, his lips coated with vanilla frosting.

But before Pete could answer, Ernie approached the table. The group watched in alarm as he pulled a box of matches from the pocket of his jogging bottoms.

"Ladies and ladies, I propose that we march over to the Council building with a jerry can of petrol and do the honourable thing. Who's with me?"

Malcolm and Tina raised their hands.

Tristan looked back towards the help desk and thanked his lucky stars that neither Janet or Lupin were there to witness this act of treason.

"Alright then, Guy Fawkes, how will burning down the Council save the Mad Pit?"

Ernie removed a spent match from the box and proceeded to chew it. "Obviously, Wigwam, it would be a highly visible and symbolic act of protest, wouldn't it? Send a message and all that."

Violet tossed her pencils onto the table. No one flinched; all eyes were on Ernie's matches.

"Excuse me," she whined, "but we only have fifteen minutes left of our booking and we've achieved absolutely nothing!"

Helen narrowed her eyes in disgust. "What could be more important than saving our library, Vio-LET?"

"I'm TALKING about saving our library, Helen! What would Mr.Thomas Hetherington think if he were alive? Would he be at the head of the march, lighting the match? No, of course he wouldn't! He was a Seatown man who loved his people. He was a man of enterprise. He opened the pit, created jobs and he built them this beautiful library."

"This place is actually pretty grotty, Vi," Courtney sniped, swinging a manicured nail from the patchy carpet tiles to the scuffed walls and back. "And it's named after some random girl."

Violet blew out her cheeks. "This 'grotty' library was named after the Madeleine Pit, which itself was named after Mr. Hetherington's daughter, Madeleine. Did they teach you nothing at school?"

"Alright, keep your wig on," Courtney huffed.

Everyone's attention returned to Violet.

"I think Mr. Hetherington and his daughter would want a fair fight," she said. "So that's what we're going to give the council: a fight, that's fair."

"Yes!" Pete punched the air. He'd never done that before and it felt good.

Ernie spat his cupcake wrapper onto the table. "You're not supposed to eat that bit, are you?"

Tristan shook his head in despair. But there was a ghost of a smile on his lips.

***

Janet and Lupin arrived from their community safety meeting to a library floor fizzing with insurrection and littered with cake crumbs.

"Summat fishy is going on, Lup," Janet whispered, as they wound their way around the book stacks and back to the front desk.

Lupin needed a cigarette and a spot of calm. Maybe she could nip around the back and savour a quiet meditative puff by the bins. *Smoking really doesn't suit me.*

"What, worse than Councillor Mitchell wanting to arm the special constables?"

Janet laughed and it felt good. Momentarily, at least.

"No, lass, there's a smell of rebellion in here. Violet's over there fuming and Pete's hiding behind the front desk looking guilty."

Lupin's shoulders slumped. "They all know, don't they?"

"Sadly, yes," Janet replied, reaching for her *Vulpine Vamp.* "So, what are we to do about it?"

Lupin shook her head. "Before we do anything, I think we could all do with a drink."

Janet nodded, emboldened by her fresh coat of lipstick. "I'm making an executive decision. To the pub."

"After work though, eh? I've got a dozen family reading packs to make up first."

They both smiled and pretended that everything was fine.

Chapter Seven

Lupin sat cross-legged on a floor strewn with multi-coloured beasts.

She placed a soft giraffe into a pretty quilted bag that accommodated a plush elephant, a lego set and two vibrantly illustrated children's books. She loved doing this little job. It offered a mini slice of tranquility away from dusty books, strip lighting and Ernie's well-intentioned insults. *I think young Rhiannon has reserved this pack. Josh will love it, he's mad for animals. And they'll not pretend to have lost the elephant. Why does everyone want to keep the elephant? The giraffe is by far the cutest.*

Without warning, an icy black gloom crept over the library manager. Janet's office was seriously bothering her chakras.

This is a first.

Zipping up her chenille cardigan, Lupin scanned the dimly-lit room.

Her eyes lit upon something strange, an object out of place.

On her hands and knees, she made her way to a mouldy old box.

"Bugger all hell!" she yelped, scattering a piece of lego to the far corner of the room. It was a zebra. "Damn family packs are murder on the knees. Begone tiny zebra, enjoy your freedom until the next set of sticky fingers finds you."

Lupin hunkered down by the box. Laughing, she pulled open the crumbling flaps and plucked out a sheaf of paper.

Over the next twenty minutes her expression shifted from bemused to worried.

"I'm gonna need a spell and a pint of snakebite."

***

Two men sat in a sleek, black car. The Mercedes-Benz C-Class was strategically parked far enough away from the Madeleine Pit library so as not to draw suspicion but close enough for its shortsighted inhabitants to be nosey.

"Ian?" asked a portly tanned man sporting soft leather toffee-coloured driving gloves.

"Yes, Norman?"

Imagine a large man in a tight suit trying to make himself look larger. "Councillor Roach to you. We might be conducting covert business but rules of engagement should be upheld."

Ian sighed as discreetly and politely as he could. "Yes, Councillor Roach?"

"Library staff appear to be leaving their place of work ten minutes early and heading directly to the 'Drunken Sailor'. Would I be right?"

Ian glanced across the street to see Janet, Tristan and Pete traipse into the pub. Even he, a man with as many layers as a sheet of A4 printing paper, could recognise the despair that radiated from them.

"Yes, you are," he responded glumly, turning to face his superior. "I thought we were going to talk about that team leader job for my Tyler?"

Norman screwed up his face in disgust. "You're always thinking of you and yours, aren't you, Thin Ian? This is a major turning point in the fortunes of our great town. What could be more important?"

"I'd appreciate it if you'd not comment on my weight, Mr Roach," Ian snapped, briefly sweeping his eyes over the elected member's well-fed form.

Norman magnanimously chose to ignore the slight on his title but couldn't ignore the assumption that he was fat. "And *I'd* appreciate it if you didn't look at me like that, you little twerp!"

Ian closed his eyes and rolled them furiously. "We've been sat here for ages. Were you hoping that Janet would close the library early?"

Ignoring him, the Councillor pressed a little button and watched the passenger window slide down.

"I think things are getting a little heated, Ian. Why don't you cool down while I continue our surveillance."

Ian shivered as the cool coastal breeze whipped its way through the sedan.

In a cafe across the street two women sat by a large picture window enjoying an unobstructed view of the quarrelling men.

"Silly gadgies, those two are," remarked Hazel, carefully removing her red woollen hat.

Maeve nursed her cappuccino and nodded. "So far up their own arses they'll never notice us sitting here judging them."

Hazel laughed into her decaf tea. "So, how's life at the Pit? Anything I should be aware of?"

"Funny you should mention that, Hazel," Maeve said. "Ernie lugged in a mouldy box t'other day."

A young waitress approached with two plates, each bearing a huge fruit scone and a ramekin filled with creamy, golden butter.

"Ta, love," Hazel said, accepting the oven-warm scones. "Is he still tinkling in the sink?"

Maeve gurned. "Yes, God help him, he's got a bad prostate. To be fair he mostly rinses after himself."

"Could be worse."

"Yeah."

Hazel spread a pat of rich butter over her scone. "So, Ernie's box. What happened to it?"

Maeve peered out at Messrs Roach and Nicholson. They were clearly arguing.

"Apparently, Tristan took it. But last time I checked it was sitting in Janet's office, gathering dust."

"That's skin."

"What?"

"Dust is skin, lass," Hazel declared.

"I know that, Hazel. I just wish you'd waited until I'd finished my scone before reminding me."

Hazel shook her head. "That poor Janet has far too much on her plate. I saw her walk into a post box the other day."

"She did what?"

"Yeah, and she was mumbling summat about Maltesers. Poor lass."

Maeve devoured the last morsel of scone then wiped her hands on a clean white serviette. "That was nice. The La'al Teacake does the scones now, did you know that?'

Hazel whispered, "Of course I do, I've still got all my teeth, haven't I?"

———————— *** ————————

"So, what happens now? Do we go in?"

Ian was desperate to get out of the car. As fancy pants as it appeared on the outside, the interior stank of steak bakes and an old man's bitterness.

"Yes, Ian, we do. Can you do that without drawing too much attention to yourself?"

Ian sighed. There'd be no talk of Tyler's job today. He'd let himself get sucked into one of Norman's daft schemes. Again.

"I suppose so," he complained. "Isn't this all a bit, you know, underhand?"

Norman laughed at his accomplice. "Marra, if you only knew how much we stand to make from this crumbling heap. Opening a building with a key is NOT 'underhand'! Capisce?"

"Capeesh, Norman."

———————— *** ————————

Janet, Tristan and Pete huddled around a small table, each nursing a drink the colour of de-icer.

"No pints tonight, folks. Tonight calls for sugar and lime slices," Janet announced, jostling for space between Tristan and Pete. "Sorry guys, my elbows do their own thing when they're tipsy."

The 'Drunken Sailor' was dotted with solo men spending their pensions on pints of bitter. Under the dart board a couple of young women cradled gin and lemonades that sloshed in glasses as big as fish bowls. They seemed confused, brows furrowed as they watched the dark geriatric debauchery unfold.

"Pete. Pete!" Janet's elbow went into overdrive as she nudged the pale apprentice.

"Um, yes?" Pete drained his cocktail and waited for the inevitable humiliation.

"Lasso over there is giving you the eye," Janet claimed, raising her eyebrows in the style of Sidney James impersonating Groucho Marx.

Pete looked over at the gin-swilling duo. The petite brunette did appear to be looking at him but it was more of a pleading gaze than a 'come hither' look. Like she wanted rescuing by someone, anyone, under the age of twenty-five.

"Nah, I think she's just come to the wrong pub, Janet."

Tristan slammed his glass on the table and stood up. "Where's Lupin when we need her?" he boomed. "She should be burning some shage, shaving all of our jobs and then, eh, flying off on her broomshtick."

"Sit down, Tristan, you're drunk." Janet patted his seat and Tristan fell on it with a thump. "She'll be here after she finishes up the family packs."

"We're only two rounds in," said Pete, who was only marginally drunk and feeling quite grown up, though he had a feeling his lips were stained.

Janet nodded. "Tristan doesn't normally do cocktails but these are trying times, lad. Be gentle on him, and wipe that blue curacao from your mouth."

A cold draft slapped Janet's ankles. Looking up she watched Lupin march through the pub towards them, flinging drunk pensioners hither and thither. Seatown's resident white witch was practically electric, her whole body radiating energy.

She looked thirsty.

Janet pawed Tristan's shirt sleeve. "Tristan, go get Lupin a pint of snakebite."

Pete looked down at his Blue Lagoon. *I could have had a proper drink.*

"I think there's a knack to this, Councillor Roach."

Norman wiggled his hand, the small metal key growing hot against his fingers. "Honestly, you'd think facilities would have replaced this lock long ago."

"Yeah, you'd think," Ian grinned. Ian was proud of his self-awareness. He knew he worked for a mildly corrupt, money-pinching system and had accepted it a long time ago. Not everyone was evil in Seatown Council, only the influential ones, those with lots of fingers in lots of pies, the men and women who never took their eyes off the ball. They were impossible to catch. And they were charismatic, almost but not quite, sincere community-loving servants of the people.

Unused to conducting dirty dealings in broad daylight the men turned out to face the street, preparing to allay passing suspicion with a wave and a, 'how do?'

Instead they were met with the beady eyes of Hazel Wilcox and Maeve Mills.

***

"Well, would you look at that, Maeve?" Hazel said, putting her hat on.

"I knew that daft beggar wouldn't manage the door."

"Tell me again how you knew they'd be here? Were you snooping in his office?"

"Course I was, chick," she replied, gathering up her coat. "I was cleaning on Wednesday and had a la'al snoop in this desk diary. He's never got used to that tablet so I knew he'd still be writing everything down. He don't trust the admin to make his appointments and he'd never dream that the cleaner would have any interest in his business."

"I'll go and pay up while you keep an eye on Abbott and Costello."

"Stay right there, Hazel. They've seen us and now they're playing statues."

Together, the women walked over to the window. Norman and Ian were standing stock-still by the library door, Norman with key in hand, Ian with hand in pocket, both working hard to look nonchalant. Maeve could see that Norman was itching to reclaim dominance, to turn and enter the library, but the moment was lost.

"Don't break your gaze, lass."

"Not me, Maeve. I love a good staring contest."

$$***$$

"Do we know them?" Norman didn't often look at women over the age of fifty, unless he was opening a care home or visiting a craft group; then he'd switch on the Roach charm.

"Why are they looking at us like that? Do you think they're onto us?" Ian asked, stumbling back into the darkened doorway.

"No, Ian, they're just nosey biddies. It fills the day in for them, eh?"

Norman dropped the key into his jacket pocket. "Come on, we'll come back another time. When it's darker."

Relief spread over Ian's face. "Suits me. I've got to pick up something for tea anyway, best be on my way before the queue at the chippy picks up."

Norman tutted and left Ian to his search for a fish supper. *How can that skinny beggar eat chips and still look like a pull through for a rifle?*

The elected representative dumped his padded behind onto the plush front seat of his sedan and pulled out into the early evening traffic. Of course, he didn't indicate.

"You got me a snakebite and black, Tristan," said Lupin, gazing into the violet-coloured pint.

Tristan threw back his head and laughed. "It'sh your fave colour, Lup, in't it? Purple, like?"

Pete glanced at Lupin's aubergine wool cardigan and the mauve alice band that pulled thick black curls away from her flushed face. *He has a point. I like drunk Tristan.*

Janet thumped the table. "Shurrup, Tristan. Knock that back, Lup and tell us what's got you all riled up."

Lupin demolished her drink. "Is my mouth all purple?" she asked, wiping her face with the back of her hand.

"Yes, lass, yes it is. Now, let's be having it!"

Just as Lupin was putting on her game face, a shadow loomed from the table behind. "Would the lot of yous SHUDDUP! I don't come 'ere to listen to chitter chatter, I come here to DRINK!"

Pete recoiled as the lumpy shape sprayed him with Tetley's bitter.

Lupin stood and grabbed a badly-dressed man by the lapels of his shiny grey suit jacket. "I'll have you know that I possess information about Seatown that would blow your tiny little mind, Bert Braithwaite! And you'll be hearing none of it!"

Bert backed off. "Away lass, what do you know about anything other than conjuring Satan and letting that cat of yours do its business in my garden!"

"Garden, Bert? You don't have a garden, you have a health hazard!"

"Yeah, because your evil familiar has fouled it up!"

They turned as Janet's stool fell to the floor with a clatter.

Stumbling between the pair, she removed a tube of *Blood Passion* from her pocket and expertly swiped her lips with a shade once deemed too scandalous for the Seatown Methodist church. Bert and Lupin, enthralled by the ritual, returned to their respective seats in silence.

"Bert, I appreciate your frankly ridiculous desire to drink in silence in a very public place but we have business to attend to…"

"That devil cat's turds are all over my…"

"… therefore if you don't zip it I'll have Sheila from Environmental Health come over and place an order on your back yard tip. Do you hear me, young man?"

Bert glugged back the remains of his bitter. "Aye, Janet. Whatever."

Janet plastered on a winning Mona Lisa smile, like a beatific, drunk angel. "Thank you, Bert. Now Lupin,…"

"But you've gorra stop prancing about outside in the middle of the night, Lupin. It puts me in bad fettle!" Bert pleaded to the back of Lupin's head.

The gin cradlers took this as their cue to escape to more youthful pastures and fled the bar in a waft of Miss Dior. Upon realising he was now the youngest person there, Pete's heart fell into his Timberland's.

"Oh my Goddess, Bert," Lupin hissed. "If you've been spying on my moon rituals I'll turn your knackers into succulents!"

"Suck your what?" the man said, turning to his rapt audience. "Did you hear that? This is verging on pornographic!"

Pete felt he had to say something. "Sir, would you like another pint?"

"And what's a child doing in the pub at this time of night?" Bert asked no-one in particular.

***

Lupin was wired. "Tristan, Seatown was a den of iniquity, heaving with pirates and my family was right in the thick of it."

Five rounds and six bags of cheese and onion crisps later, Janet, Tristan, Lupin and Pete blearily emerged from the most entertaining team meeting in recent memory. It was on a par with the time Tristan's ex-girlfriend had stormed the kitchen during a budget review and spooned strawberry yogurt onto his head. But more surreal.

The clank of a dusty bell announced last orders.

"How long have we been here?" Janet queried, blinking.

"Hours. I've losht all feeling in my mouth," Tristan complained, running a blue tongue over sugar-encrusted teeth.

Pete had moved on to Diet Coke. He knew his limits and respected them, something his older colleagues, for the life of them, couldn't comprehend. *The lonely, sober life of a Gen Z.*

Chapter Eight

Monday arrived and with it a boisterous craft club.

Violet arrived first, clad in her sturdiest boots and armed with a flip chart. It took two attempts to tumble through the revolving door and to her shame she was met with an audience.

"Do you require assistance, madame?" Ernie asked, springing from his chair to grab the flip chart.

Violet politely shook him off, desperate to keep her new woollen winter jacket clean. It was dry-clean only, she dreaded wearing it and bemoaned the day Marks and Sparks had hypnotised her into buying such an inconveniently beautiful garment.

"Are you our new door man, Ernie? Not much of a uniform is it?" she remarked, hobbling over to the craft club table, determined not to tumble in front of a man.

Ernie grabbed the flip chart from Violet's cold hands and parked it against Sport/ Biographies.

"You lot could make me a uniform. Nice pair of pants, smart jacket. I'd be a new man!"

Tina followed, one hand balancing a large tupperware container stuffed with devil's food cake, the other gripping a cloth bag filled with felt tip pens, printer paper and post-it notes.

Malcolm and Helen arrived together, raising a total of four eyebrows.

Helen, resplendent in a silk pinafore (*Cement Gris*), linked arms with Malcolm but not in a romantic sense, only to keep him upright.

Malcolm was mourning.

"Come on Mal, we're not closed yet," Helen whispered into his ear, making sure to leave a trace of nude lipstick, (*Mud Chic).*

Violet didn't bite because she was preoccupied with keeping Ernie's hands off the legs of her flip chart. "Ernie, I'm more than capable of putting this up, thank you very much."

Ernie knelt by Violet's ankles. "I need you to spread 'em, Vi."

"Excuse me?" she squealed, jumping away from the man's grasping fingers. "Do you want me to put Tristan onto you?"

"Well, I'd prefer Janet but…"

Shrugging off her coat, taking great care to keep the luxury garment as far from Ernie's reach as humanly possible, Violet dropped onto all fours with a grunt.

"Hello, Vi. I meant the flipchart legs."

"Hmm, yes."

"But your gams are shapely enough now that I'm close up, like."

Violet slapped the air between her and Ernie. "I'll have you know I carry a corkscrew for protection!"

"Good for you, lass. Now, let's knock this tripod into shape."

***

Flip-chart successfully erected, Violet smoothed her clothes and faced her audience. Ernie had returned to his seat, but to her dismay was edging his way into the inner circle. Tina was offering him a slice of chocolate cake. *We've not even started and that hussy's already feeding the five thousand.* Ernie accepted the wedge of cocoa and sugar with glee, muttering something about the breakfast of champions.

"Can I have your attention, please?" Violet implored, in a raised voice that was just-about-acceptable for a library.

Malcolm rapped the table. "Settle, everyone. Vi's going to tell us how we can save the library, aren't you, Vi?"

***

Lupin deftly sliced the banana with a swiftness that unnerved Pete. "Ernie literally threw four boxes of

77

angel slices onto the counter, Janet," she moaned, tossing the mushy fruit into a bowl of bran flakes. "Pushed in front of poor Mrs. Fee, too."

Janet was brushing her hair over the kitchen sink. "My bob never sits properly when I'm hungover. It's all skew whiff."

"You're still hungover?" Pete asked, munching on an out of date angel slice. "It's been three days!"

The door swung open.

"Have I had a weekend, lads and lasses," Tristan announced, marching into the kitchen, which took all of two strides.

Janet turned from the sink to face him. "Really, Tristan? Do tell. Did a bevvy of beauties take up residence in your bedsit?"

"Bevvy of beauties? Are you writing for the Daily Star now, Jan?" he smirked. "Even better; it seems our boring old Seatown was once a hotbed of debauchery and vice."

Lupin looked up from her breakfast. "Did you go through the haul? I thought you thought I was crackers?"

"I did, kind of. And I do," he grinned, chucking a damp tea towel at her. "That box of musty old paper just might save us. I've brought it back here for a proper look through but from what I've already seen there's a lot to unpack."

Janet repressed a hopeful thought; it was just too soon for that kind of malarkey. "Even though it's highly likely we're descended from murderous criminals? Sorry, Lup."

Tristan shrugged. "It's worth the risk, Jan, because we're running out of ideas. But I'm going to need help sorting it out and proving its authenticity."

Lupin chucked the banana skin into the sink and returned to her breakfast. "You know just the man."

THUMP, THUMP.

"Behave yourselves, I'm coming in!"

Lupin's bran flakes jumped from her spoon and scattered over the table. "For the love of Hecate!"

Tristan tutted and backed himself against the door.

"I can't seem to get in!" Violet bellowed. "What's blocking me?"

"We've, eh, got a new filing cabinet, Vi," Janet said, muffling giggles. "Not much space for anyone other than staff at the minute. What do you need?"

The team heard a distinct, 'humpf'. "My markers have run dry. Can you spare a black, a blue and a green? We're starting our campaign today."

"What campaign?" Tristan inquired, gripping the door frame with his bony fingers.

"We're saving the library, you ninny. Now can you please get away from the door and check your stationery cupboard? There were plenty of markers last time I checked!"

"The cheek of *her*!" Lupin laughed. "Pete, climb into that cupboard and fetch her some markers. Not the new ones though."

"Bless her," Janet smiled. "I wonder what they're planning?"

Tristan nimbly crept back to the table, whispering, "I imagine it'll involve Vi talking the ear off the Council until they cry and surrender. Or, they'll close us early as punishment."

"I heard that, young man!"

Pete ratcheted around in the stationery cupboard, retrieving the crucial markers. "Tristan, can you give them to her?"

"Yes, lad. Hand them over."

Tristan inched open the door and was met with Vi's looming, exasperated face. "Ooh, hello, Vi. You been there long?"

'Very funny, Tristan," she snapped, grabbing the markers. "We're only trying to help."

Tristan grinned. "Violet, we wouldn't be without you."

"Well, it's nice to be appreciated." Violet's beaming face lit up the cramped doorway.

As Tristan gently pushed the door shut, he said, "Don't let the door smack you on the way out, ta-ra!"

Janet spat out her tea. "Tristan, you demon!"

Tristan clapped his hands. "Right, where were we?"

———————— *** ————————

"Alright lass, where's the fire?" Ernie asked Vi, removing a box of matches from his pocket. "Did I start it?"

Violet power-walked towards the campaign group, cheeks puffed and fist raised in the air. "They're hiding something!"

Before anyone could respond, a blast of cold air suddenly swept over the group.

"Bloody pirates live in bloody Seatown!"

They all turned to watch a wind-blown Courtney swing through the door and sling her backpack onto Malcolm's lap. Her cheeks were scarlett and her lips were blue.

"Courtney," Helen scoffed, "is that lipstick you're wearing or have we been teleported to the arctic circle?"

"It's lippie from the market stall your Steph runs, Helen. Seatown's Next Top Model, eh?"

Violet tutted loudly and crossed her arms. "Excuse me ladies but let's leave the cat fight to another day, shall we?"

Tina bravely took the high ground. "Can we please get back to Courtney's pirates? Unless you have something to add, Ernie?"

Ernie looked right through Tina, deep in his own thoughts. "I knew a pirate once," he reminisced. "Sold me a dodgy Downton Abbey box set that were in Spanish."

Courtney was bouncing up and down on the balls of her hot pink Converse. "Well, mam was in the 'Drunken ' the other night and she said *that* lot were in, knocking back cocktails and being dead loud."

Tina raised her hand. "They're entitled to a drink, love. It's stressful working with the public. I should know, I've had to bake for the most awful people. Once someone smacked me on the back of the head with a rocky road."

Malcolm empathised. "I'm very sorry to hear that, Tina. The biddies at the home are just as bad. I've had urine…"

"Shurrup and listen to her!" Violet shouted, the thread veins on her cheeks flashing red. "This is no time for flirting!"

Suitably mollified, everyone's attention returned to Courtney. "Go on then, lass," Violet urged. "We're all ears."

Ernie rattled his box of matches by Malcom's head. "Aye, Malcolm hasn't grown into his ears yet, have you lad? Like two rusty wingnuts."

Courtney stamped her feet. "Hello?" she bawled. "I've got 'Interview Skills' at 11 o'clock and if I'm late again all the pink wafers will be gone."

Ernie crossed his arms and nodded towards the girl. "Come on, scoundrels. Stop giving her a hard time and listen."

"Thanks Ernie?" Courtney responded, eyes screwed up with suspicion.

"Love, I'm busting for a wee so get it out before I evacuate in front of the elderly."

The table disintegrated into tuts and groans.

"Anyway, mam was necking jager bombs with her FWB when she heard Loopy Lup talking about pirates."

Malcolm looked puzzled. "Sorry, what's a FWB?"

"Don't go there, Malcolm," Violet scolded, much to Courtney's amusement.

"Lupin started talking about how Seatown used to be full of criminals, pirates and the like," she continued, arms flailing with excitement. "Apparently she read about it from some manky documents she found."

Tina was agog. "Pirates, how exciting! So, what else did she hear?"

Courtney shrugged. "Dunno, mam went to the bar for another round and got chatting to her ex."

Ernie barked a loose, phlegm-filled cough. "What documents are you talking about, lass?"

Courtney didn't try to disguise her disgust. "You're rank, Ernie. I think it was that gross box of paper you brought in a while back. Did you not have a look inside? You're nosey enough."

Ernie's grimy hands smoothed trousers that were shiny with dirt. "Not really, our Court. What I did see were ancient Seatown street maps and what looked like old meeting minutes. Very dull. No boobies. Perfect for Twistam."

Violet was oddly contemplative. "Courtney, this is all very entertaining but I can't see how these old papers are going to help our campaign. Do you?"

Courtney was chuffed at having an elder request her opinion. It was a rare event. Tutors only spoke to her to complain about the quality of her work or to ask her to get off her phone.

"Yeah, but what if there's treasure? There might be gold buried somewhere!" *I could get mam some proper extensions* and *have my lunch in Wetherspoons, every day.*

Violet approached the flipchart and started writing with her blue marker. "Cheapskates. This marker barely works! Can you all read that?"

Helen squinted. "Erm, does it say, 'How to Sell our Library?'"

"No madam, it doesn't. It says, 'How to Save our Library'. Why would we want to sell it?"

With a deep sadness Malcolm popped the last morsel of chocolate cake into his mouth. "Vi, did you not say that the staff were hiding something?"

Violet sneered. "Yes, they looked sneaky and they couldn't get me out fast enough."

"Nothing new there, Vi," Helen spat.

Violet swivelled to her flipchart. "Did someone speak? No? Alright then, I've got two words for you: fund raiser!"

Ernie raised a sticky hand. "That's one word, lass. And I know how we can save this mouldy old dump."

Violet sighed into her poly-blend blouse. "For crying out loud, Ernie, I was about to break us into discussion groups."

Everyone else looked at Ernie expectantly.

"I go to the 'La'al Teacake' every day at closing for Eileen's leftovers," he whispered. "Celeste loves a chunk of plumbread for supper."

Malcolm scrunched up his face. "Who's Celeste?"

"My pet rat, not that it's important. Right, so a Brinks van stops outside The Cumbria Bank across the road at five past five on a Tuesday and a Friday. I propose that we rob the Brinks van. I know Andy, the driver and he's just had a vasectomy so he's got an awful limp and he'd never catch up with Courtney."

"Why me? I can't rob or run to save myself!"

Ernie looked confused. "Can you see Helen or Malcolm legging it up the high street with a bag of swag?"

Violet tapped her marker against the flipchart. "Time to get serious people, there'll be no robbing banks. Helen would trip over her costume jewelry, for starters."

Malcolm slapped the table with both hands. "Violet made a funny!"

"Shhh, Tristan's coming!" Tina screeched.

Tristan offered vague greetings to the group, then made a beeline for Ernie. "Young man, can we have a word in the office?"

Ernie looked worried. "Tristan lad, I were only joking about the bank robbery."

***

Ernie squeezed into the hot and steamy kitchen.

"Would you like a cup of tea, Ernie?" Pete asked, muscle memory replacing an overwhelming desire to run outside and gulp a cubic litre of fresh air.

Pete felt bad but he didn't want Ernie lurking in the small space. He couldn't identify the scent that radiated from the older man but it was a confusing combination of wee and talc.

"No lad, I'm already cradling a full bladder and that would tip me into indecency," the man replied without a hint of irony. "You're not going to be long, are you?"

Tristan smiled. "Ernie, lad, how do you fancy helping me go through that old box of papers you brought us? You know more about Seatown than anyone."

Hopping from one foot to the other, Ernie considered Tristan's proposition. "Well, it would depend on when, Tristan. I've got bingo on Mondays and Wednesdays and I sit by the harbour every other night."

"Can you spare tomorrow evening, after closing? I'm sure the harbour could manage and I'll buy the fish and chips."

Ernie nodded. "Aye, that'll do. But get supper from Marconi's, not the Saveloy."

"Great stuff, Ernie," Janet said, rising from her chair and showing him to the door. "We've got official library madness to talk about now."

"See you at 5.30pm and not a minute earlier," Tristan shouted after the older man.

"Aye lad, I'll have my secretary Davinia put it in my filofax."

Chapter Nine

"Right, Tristan and I are going to see Amanda over in Seatown House. Should we tell her about the documents? Does she need to know about the pirates?"

Pete nibbled on a crunch cream. "I don't know anything about Seatown pirates because I'm not into old stuff but shouldn't people already know about this?"

"He's right," Tristan said. "How come none of us knew about our town's supposed criminal history?"

"Because it's embarrassing," Lupin mumbled, placing her empty cereal bowl into the sink.

With a barely concealed sigh Janet reached over and filled Lupin's bowl with warm water. "Aye, maybe. It's not something I'd want to broadcast to all and sundry."

"Meaning the posh Cumbrians in Ambleside," Tristan remarked.

"My nan's from Ambleside and she's lovely," Pete mumbled, his face pink.

"You ready, Tristan?" Squinting at her reflection in the kettle, Janet carefully painted her lips with a passive-aggressive shade of fuschia pink.

Tristan raised his eyebrows. "Watch out, Amanda, Janet Sowerby means business!"

***

Janet and Tristan walked into the library garage towards the parked van. Emblazoned on one side of the grubby vehicle was the bright blue and green Seatown Council logo, an abstract representation of verdant Cumbrian fells and icy, coastal waters; the other boasted a busted wheel arch, as crumpled as Ernie's shabby suit trousers.

"I call shotgun!" Tristan exclaimed with a wink.

Janet pulled a face. "You mean you want me to drive."

"Yes please," he nodded. "Otherwise, I'll have to drive through reception and crush Terry before he can offer me another duff Ralex watch."

"Fair enough," she said. "But I owe him for Avon so we'll need to stop for cash on the way."

***

"Janet. Tristan," said the thin-lipped young man with fashionably mussed up brown hair.

Tristan nodded, eyes glued to the floor. "Alright, marra?"

Janet approached the reception desk, gripping her purse. "Terry, love, here's a twenty for my Avon."

"How's that nude lip gloss working out for you?" he asked, stuffing the note into his trouser pocket. "Bit of a change, eh?"

"If Seatown weren't so bleeding windy, I'd wear it all the time, Tel," Janet complained. "But I'm spending more time picking hair out of my mouth than I'd like, it's so sticky. You don't sell industrial strength hairspray, do you?"

Terry leaned forward, arms resting on the fake teak countertop. "Under the reception stuff, you mean?"

"We're going to be late, Jan," Tristan grumbled, tapping his foot on the worn brown carpet.

Janet turned back towards her colleague. "Sir, yes, sir. Tel, I'll give you a ring later."

"You do that, Jan," said the wiley receptionist. "Sorry your watch broke, Tristan. I told you not to wear it in bright or artificial light but you wouldn't listen."

Tristan shook his head and scowled. "I'm not a vampire, Terry, I need to know the time when I'm awake. You know, during the day."

"Well, that's the risk you take when you buy dodgy stuff from a receptionist," Terry replied. "Enjoy your meeting with Mad Manda!"

_____ *** _____

This time Amanda was ready.

On her desk was a mint green document wallet brimful of incriminating documentation.

Sometimes she liked to stroke it; delicately lifting its soft flap to gaze at the tantalising contents within.

Amanda already felt like a winner.

_____ *** _____

As Janet and Tristan approached the open plan office, Barry materialised from the kitchenette. In his hands was a tray bearing a stainless steel teapot that was destined to leak, four mugs, a bowl of damp sugar, a tiny jug of milk, and a selection of chocolate biscuits.

"Lovely to see you both!" he chirped.

Janet offered him the faintest of smiles. "Choccie biccies, must be really bad news."

Ignoring her, Barry nudged Amanda's door open with his bum, placed the tray on her desk then retreated to a dark corner whereupon he pulled a small notebook and pen from his jacket pocket. Janet was mesmerised by his grace. *He could have been a figure skater in another life, the little twit.*

In a clumsy attempt at diplomacy, Amanda had squashed three chairs around a small circular table. Janet noticed that the woman was sitting on her office chair which elevated her four inches above everyone else. *She can't help herself, always having to lord it.*

"Morning, Janet and Tristan. Shall I be mother?" Amanda asked, picking up the teapot.

Tristan grimaced. "Thanks, mum. Milk and two sugars, please."

"Oh, Tristan, you're hilarious," Amanda trilled, pouring tea into thick white mugs. "Take a biscuit and a seat."

As Janet sat down, her eyes lit on the green folder. *That's us in there. We're in that folder.*

The soft chocolate digestive immediately disintegrated in Tristan's mouth. "Amanda, why have you got four mugs out?"

"Well...."

The office door flew open and slammed against the flimsy partition wall. Amanda's *Kittens and Puppies* calendar jumped from its pin and swept to the floor.

"Sorry I'm late," Councillor Norman Roach shouted, heading straight for the biscuits. "God, these are terrible," he mumbled, spitting crumbs into the milk jug.

Amanda diligently stood up. "Welcome, Councillor Roach."

"Miss Amanda Love," he announced, wiping chocolate from his mouth. "I'll give you a man to love, eh lass?"

"I'd rather clean my lugs with a letter opener," she muttered.

"What was that?"

"I said it's lovely to see you, Councillor!"

"Would you like me to minute that, Amanda?" Barry chirped from his dark corner.

Norman spun around to address the minute taker. "I was only joking, lad. Anyway, we've not started yet."

The man eyed Amanda's roomy ergonomic chair then plopped down beside Janet. "Well, Janet, enjoying your visit to control centre?"

Janet edged to the side of her seat. "I'm thrilled, Norman, although it's a pity it's not under better circumstances."

"Who've we got here then? Is this your secretary?" the man asked a scowling Tristan, who instinctively spread his legs a little further apart.

Amanda was losing the room. "Okay, let's get started. Janet, Tristan, we're here to officially announce that the library will close in three months.

That should give you enough time to signpost people to other local services."

"Don't know why we have to wait," Norman grumbled.

"Excuse me?" Janet asked.

"Don't shoot the messenger, Janet," he pleaded, holding both hands up, palms out, in front of his chest. "But I think we can all agree that people from Seatown prefer Twittering to reading."

"That's not true and you know it," Tristan interjected. "The library is a community hub, loved and needed by many."

Norman tutted. "That's a nice speech and all but half empty community hubs cost money."

"We also provide training, support and internet access for those that don't have it," Tristan explained. "It doesn't matter to us if hundreds are coming through the doors or not. It's a public service."

Janet heard faint clapping emerge from Barry's corner. *He's still a twit but, bless.*

"What was that, Barry?" Amanda asked, infuriated at this flagrant defiance.

"Swatting a fly, boss."

Tristan wasn't finished. "Books are the lifeblood of well, life. Learning should be free for everyone and that means a library facility in every town and village in Cumbria."

Neither was Norman. "Books? What can anyone learn from Fifty Shades of Twilight that they can't pick up after an honest day's graft?"

Janet groped for her lipstick but it wasn't in her pocket. "We're not here to discuss Norman's reading habits. Can we please move on?"

"It's Councillor Roach, young lady!"

Amanda opened the mint green folder and fanned out a number of printed sheets. *This'll shut them up.*

"I'm sorry, Janet but we've got the proof right here in front of us."

Janet briefly scanned the documents and shook her head. "I know the figures, I sent these to you, Amanda."

"So, why are you fighting this?" Amanda was baffled; statistics, dodgy or otherwise, were the foundation of local government decision-making.

"Because we're not talking about numbers," Janet stressed. "We're talking about Violet, a woman who has single-handedly established eleven different hobby clubs that between them have had over one hundred members."

Tristan nodded frantically. "Our employability classes have helped twenty-six young people find work in the last year. Our local history section has so much potential. Just last week Ernie brought us a box full of historical documents…"

"Tristan." Janet made a small slashing gesture that nobody missed.

"What documents?" Norman and Amanda asked.

"Oh, nothing," Janet mumbled. "Just something Ernie found in a skip."

"That tramp shouldn't be allowed in the library," Norman huffed. "I'm positive I saw him gob on my Merc once, and I can get the CCTV footage to prove it."

The awkward silence that followed was broken by a ringing phone.

Relieved, Amanda shot over to her desk. "Sorry, I'll just grab this."

Norman leaned in towards Janet. "What's with these documents? Is it something we should know about?"

"Who's 'we', Councillor?"

"The people who write the cheques, *Mizz* Sowerby."

Janet jumped as Amanda slammed down her phone.

"Well, then," she said to no-one in particular, her complexion like spoiled cream. "I think we're done for today."

"We're clearly not!" Norman shouted, getting to his feet. "I need a closing date right now."

Amanda snatched up her stress ball and bit into it.

"What's going on, Amanda?" Janet felt a flicker of hope.

Amanda blinked. "According to Pauline Graves, the library will remain open until more supporting information can be gathered."

Norman slammed a meaty fist onto Amanda's desk. "No date? What does that mean? Who does she think she is?"

"Director of Community Services," Barry confirmed. "Do I minute all of this?"

"Yes, Baz," Amanda sighed.

Chapter Ten

Lupin gathered up her bag, keys and coat before pulling open the front door and heading out into the cold, dark night.

The scent of lavender followed her as she stepped onto the cool, dimly-lit street. She had doused herself with a home-made spray concoction after an unsatisfactory bath that had left her as relaxed as a clenched fist. *Maybe recreational drugs* are *all they're cracked up to be.*

A cabal of grubby eight year-old boys kicked a ball between parked cars. "Alright, Loopy? Where are you off to?" asked Jordan, the clear leader by at least two inches.

"Hiya, Jordy, shouldn't you be inside doing your homework?"

A tiny dark-haired lad shoved his way to the front of the group. "I've already done his homework, miss. So he could come out and play footie."

Jordan will be on Council in twenty years' time.

"Is that so?" she asked. "Well, I'd better rush. I'm off to my mam and dad's house."

"They're hippies, aren't they? Your mam and dad?" Jordan asked, his chin raised.

Lupin pulled her purple wool coat tightly around her. "Do you know what a hippy is, Jordan?"

Jordan looked to his gang for clues but none were forthcoming. "They eat vegetables all the time. And they don't cut their hair."

"Spot-on, lad. Can I go now?"

Jordan nodded and Lupin swept up the street in a mist of herbal fragrance.

***

After a bracing twenty-minute walk, Lupin arrived at her parent's modest semi on the outskirts of Seatown. From the outside it was deceptively bland, with few garden ornaments save a small grinning gnome and a stone bird bath. But inside was a different matter.

"I'm here!" Lupin shook off her coat and flung it over the bannister.

A small man sporting a soft blue collarless shirt, loose cotton trousers and moccasin slippers padded soundlessly into the hallway. "Hi love, your mam is in with Geraldine. Do you want your tea now?"

"Nice to see you too, dad," Lupin laughed, enveloping her diminutive father, Aiden, in a hug.

"Sorry, Lup, how are you?" he asked, pulling back to look at his daughter. "I can smell lavender; are you stressed?"

"To be honest, I'm not sure," she replied, walking the short distance into the kitchen.

"Hmm. Let's get you a nice cup of green tea and see where that takes you," he offered, reaching up into a scrubbed pine cupboard stocked with dozens of small, colourful boxes. He picked out a packet of loose green tea leaves and set about the ritual of tea making.

Lupin warmed her legs against the kitchen radiator. "See you've still got that awful gnome. I thought you were going to recycle it?"

Her father sighed. "Your mam wants to keep it. Says it'll protect us from real gnomes who can be nasty little buggers if you rub them up the wrong way."

"How did you get on with Geraldine?"

"Not bad, I think," he replied, handing her a cup of soothing tea. "She says I've got to keep an eye on Derek at work. Apparently he's after my job."

Lupin's father managed Seatown's famed Lighthouse Theatre, a breeding ground for energetic performers of middling ability.

"But Derek's a carpenter," Lupin laughed, taking a sip from her mug.

"Yes, a very ambitious carpenter with a troubling Gilbert and Sullivan obsession."

Lupin sank into a lumpy old armchair and sighed.

Her father frowned. "So, you said you weren't sure if you were stressed. Have you been meditating?"

She nodded. "Every day, but I don't think meditation is going to fix this."

"I see. Is it work?"

Lupin picked at a loose thread. "The library was closing and I was just getting my head around that but then today we were told we've been given more time."

Her father waited.

"Ernie found a load of old paper recently that apparently may shed light on our, er, history."

"That's interesting," he responded, with the tiniest hint of panic. "Hmm, where's my amethyst worry stone?"

Lupin pulled a pink, shiny stone from the side of the arm chair.

"Where it usually is, dad," she said, dropping the warm gem into his outstretched hand. "Look, no-one really knows about the Lawsons back in 'ye olden' days so I reckon nothing will come of it. Plus, we can't be related to all of them."

He patted his daughter's hand. "You may not know it but our family has worked really hard to make things right, Lupin. We have nothing to be ashamed of, so don't dwell on it."

As Lupin drained her tea, cackles of laughter drifted down into the kitchen, followed by a flurry of footsteps.

"Here come the trouble makers!" Lupin said, excited to see her mother and Geraldine. She turned to her father. "Don't say anything dad, not right now." He nodded his consent.

Two remarkably similar women entered the kitchen.

Both sported flowing, soft jersey dresses in rich, autumnal shades; their outfits complemented with bold costume jewelry in golds and reds, their feet shod in chunky, no-nonsense biker boots. Where Lupin's mother, Anna, rocked a dramatic hennaed pixie cut, Geraldine preferred a slightly less striking 'do, opting for long, wavy brown tresses.

After a round of hugs, Geraldine took Lupin's hand. "Are you ready, chick?"

_____ *** _____

Geraldine led Lupin into a small box room filled with flickering light. A table with two chairs was set out in the style of a romantic dinner à deux. Upon a starched white table cloth lay a deep purple silk runner; all that was missing was cutlery, steaming bowls of spaghetti and a bottle of plonk.

Behind the table on a deep window sill blazed a row of colourful candles. None of them were fragranced as Geraldine was a slave to her sinuses.

"You know, this many candles is a bit of a fire risk, Ger," Lupin said, sitting down. "Mam's nail art kits are right beside you."

Geraldine waved her away. "It's a habit, Lup. The clients love it and it makes me look ten years' younger."

"I'm embarrassed to admit that I've never *really* got the hang of reading the leaves."

"The universe is in these tea leaves," Geraldine explained, pointing to Lupin's porcelain cup. "It's all about intention and interpretation. Anyway, tarot's more your thing, right?"

Lupin nodded. "But I won't read my own. Last time I did, I convinced myself to go on a blind date with a teenage vicar and that didn't end well, did it?"

"No love, it didn't," Geraldine sympathised, settling into her seat. "But let's not dwell. Now then, have you thought of a question you want to ask the leaves?"

"Yes." Lupin knew not to divulge her query.

"I hope you've left a mouthful of tea, greedy guts. Now, get swirling."

With the remaining leaves floating inside, Lupin rotated her cup in a clockwise direction with one hand and knocked on the teak table with the other. *Can I guarantee a safe library, safe job and safe family? Too needy? Probably.* Then, after gently resting her saucer over the cup, she tipped both over and allowed the contents to settle.

As Lupin focused on positive thoughts, Geraldine was on Facebook. "Sorry love, are you done?" she asked, shoving her phone into an oversized bronze-coloured leather bag.

Lupin suppressed a giggle. "Yep, I'm ready," she said, handing over the cup. "Hit me with your witchy genius."

"Right then, let's see what the gods of Twinings have got in store for you."

She studied the cup and began to hum.

"Is that 'Wannabe'?"

Geraldine's gaze remained fixed on the scattered tea leaves. "Hush, lass," she whispered. "The Spice Girls were obviously a coven. As all spell workers should know."

Lupin mulled over this fresh information. "Riiight. So, what about B*Witched?"

"Don't be daft." And that was that.

The combination of smouldering candles and internal anguish made Lupin break out in a sweat. *Respect the process, respect the process.*

Geraldine frowned as she rotated the cup. "You've got worries, my lovely."

"Does Dolly Parton sleep on her back?" Lupin mumbled, pulling her wool sweater over her head.

Geraldine looked up. "What was that?"

"Sorry, I was boiling hot," she replied, fanning her face. "Is my stress that obvious?"

"Your aura's got a troubling tinge," Geraldine informed her. "And it's seriously clashing with your hair."

"Oh," Lupin said, patting her head.

Geraldine placed the cup back on the table. "Right then. Do you want the bad news or the okay news?"

"Go on, break out the okay news," Lupin replied, steadying herself.

"The rim of the cup is indicating a move."

"Ooh, really? To Ibiza?" Lupin crossed her toes.

"Sorry lass, not the Balearics. Any thoughts?"

"Well, I've been complaining about Bert Braithwaite to the Council so maybe they've seen sense and they're kicking him out?"

Geraldine looked pensive. "Maybe, but keep an open mind. Your mam told me the library might be closing. This could be a new start for you, eh?"

"What, going back to Finance? That's not a new start, that's going backwards. I love my job and I intend to fight for it."

"Good for you."

Lupin shuffled her chair closer to the table. "What's the bad news? Because, you know, that was pretty bad."

"Look, I'm seeing an anchor, which is generally pretty positive but my bones are telling me otherwise. Does that make sense?"

Pirates. Dodgy seafaring criminals.

"Yep." Lupin began to fidget with her charm bracelet. "Geraldine, how much do you know about our family?

Geraldine placed Lupin's cup back on its saucer and looked at her friend. "Well, I know I like you all," she said. "You're quirky, kind and you've got great taste in fortune tellers."

Lupi's shoulder's dropped. "Really?"

"Of course, chick," she reassured her. "Though Anna burns far too much patchouli incense; my airways are battered. Apart from that, you're all winners. Why?"

This wasn't going in quite the right direction. "Yes, but what do you *know* about us?"

"Your family's lived here forever and you've been hippies for generations," she began. "Oh, your mam ran a good trade in wind chimes during the nineties New Age revival..."

"Don't mention those flippin' wind chimes. I think I've got PTSD."

"...and Aiden has given hundreds of kids a start in the theatre yet still hasn't developed a serious drinking problem. You, my love, don't get paid enough for sharing your passion for books and learning. How's that for starters?"

Lupin's eyes began to water.

"That's rather dramatic, lass," Geraldine teased, pulling a clean hanky from her pocket and handing it to Lupin. "Tell your aunty Ger all about it."

"I wish you *were* my aunty," Lupin blubbed into the tissue. "Then you'd know just how bloody awful our family is."

"Do you need another tissue? Because you're turning my stomach."

"No, I'm fine but thank you," she said, firing the sopping wet tissue into her mum's craft bin. "Look, people are going to find out something very soon. It's about the Lawsons and it'll make us look *really* bad."

"Lup, if I've learned anything about fortune telling it's that there's bugger all we can do about what's already happened. All we can do is worry about what's *going* to happen."

"Yeah, that's exactly what I'm stressing about!"

"Hold on, I haven't finished."

"Soz."

"The beauty of it, chick, is that only *you* can decide what your future's going to look like."

"I don't think I've got that much say in it."

"You've got a say in how it'll make you feel. And you *can* shape it, believe me."

Lupin got up and gave Geraldine a hug. "That was very soppy of you, Geraldine. I'm shocked."

"Give over, would you," Geraldine scolded. "Now, cross my palm with silver. Or a fiver, if you have one."

Lupin pulled a crisp note from her pocket. "I know you're saving for a new crystal ball, so I'll give you a tenner. And it's still a bargain compared to how much you charge hen parties."

"We're all slaves to capitalism, doll," she laughed, taking the money. "Right, let's go and get tipsy on Anna's home-made wine."

"Not sure, Ger," Lupin scowled. "The last time I got drunk on mum's plum wine I nearly fell over the harbour wall on my way home."

Geraldine patted Lupin's back in encouragement. "You don't want to tip over into that oil-infested water.

You know, the last time I went for a walk there I saw your friend, Ernie. He was sitting on a bench by himself singing sea shanties."

Lupin shuddered. *Shiver me bloody timbers.*

Chapter Eleven

Hazel's fingers were a blur of knit one, purl one, feeding on a mountain of crimson mohair nestling on her lap. The hypnotic click-clack of bamboo needles had lulled her wife into a gentle snooze. The snoring was bearable as she was still mostly upright.

"Make us a cup of tea, would you, love?" Hazel shouted over to Jean.

"What?" she spluttered, wide eyes darting around the room, before settling on Hazel.

"Sorry, petal, I wanted to make sure you were still breathing."

"Did you now?" she asked, rubbing her eyes. "Well, I am. Does that mean I can go back to sleep?

Hazel stuck out her bottom lip. "Oh go on, Jean, I'm parched."

Jean was extremely comfy and wouldn't give up without a fight. "How about a game of rock, paper, scissors?"

"That's only for important decisions, like how much to leave the kids in our will."

"Alright, I surrender," she said, pushing herself off the sofa with a groan. "Rich Tea or choccy Hobnob?"

"Hobnob, obviously." Hazel blew her wife a kiss as she left the room.

Under the mound of wool a mobile phone beeped.

Gingerly extracting the device from her soon-to-be cardigan, Hazel peered at the message on her home screen.

"I've bought you three months xx"

"Jean, love?"

"Yes, my darling?"

"Can you bring in the whole packet? I feel a binge coming on."

"Thank you, Pauline, you won't regret it xx"

Chapter Twelve

Tristan left Marconi's jostling two portions of piping hot fish and chips, each of which had been stingily wrapped in a single layer of thin, greasy paper. *I'm going to need skin grafts at this rate.*

Before crossing the road to the library he passed a cafe, three charity shops and a black-fronted off-licence packed with cocky track-suited teenagers grasping bottles of blue WKD with skinny hands. *Good luck to them.*

Waiting for a convoy of taxis to pass, Tristan took in the library's grand three-storey Georgian symmetry. With rotten sash windows that were too important to replace and mossy slate roof tiles that served as a gull love motel, the building was decades past its sell-by date. Its sand-coloured stuccoed ground floor was dented with bike handle marks and the wheelchair ramp wouldn't have been out of place on a tough mudder obstacle course.

Moving closer, Tristan clocked a dark Ernie-shaped figure standing in the corner of the library doorway. The man's back was to the street and his hands were suspiciously absent. *Is he actually bloody serious?*

"Couldn't wait 'til I opened up, eh?"

Ernie swivelled round, clutching a slim pack of Rizla and a battered tobacco tin.

"What was that, lad?" he asked, a damp cigarette paper clinging to his lips.

Tristan unlocked the main door and knocked off the alarm. "I said, 'I hope you're hungry,' because this fish could moonlight as a draught excluder."

Ernie finished rolling his cigarette then placed it behind his ear. "I don't pee on my own doorstep, Trident," he said, nudging Tristan in the back. "Lead the way, I could eat a scabby hoss between two mattresses."

***

"You know, Janet won't appreciate the smell of greasy fish when she comes in tomorrow."

He's right, she'll kick off. Tristan popped a chip in his mouth and looked up at Ernie. "I didn't think you'd be too bothered."

Ernie looked offended. "What, you think I don't have standards?"

Tristan shook his head.

"Correct, I don't. But Janet does. Never a hair outta place, and that lipstick?"

"Do you fancy her, Ernie?"

"Away with you, lad. Just saying we could have had this in the kitchen."

"Yeah, well. The box is in here and we'll need the space to spread out."

Sat at a trestle table, opposite Tristan, Ernie speared his chips with a tarnished fork that had been in the library longer than its oldest member, (Betty Burgess, ninety-nine. Fan of Catherine Cookson and Stephen King). Tristan was surprised to find that Ernie favoured cutlery over eating with his bare hands.

"Ernie, why have you left the fish batter? That's the best bit."

"I'm going to treat Celeste."

"Your rat."

"Yeah."

"Right, how about we get started?"

***

"Do you need me to get down on the floor with you?"

"It would help, Ernie."

"Are you prepared to help me back up when we're done?"

"Course I will."

"You're one of the good ones, Tristanna."

Tristan had painstakingly organised the stack of paper according to topic, each bundle placed into a different coloured folder. From the pile of folders that lay on the floor he pulled a yellow one towards him and Ernie.

"This folder has loads of old meeting minutes in it," he announced with a grin. "We're talking about the early 1800s, so it's pretty dense."

Ernie sat cross-legged, looking more comfortable than Tristan. "Are you telling me there's stuff in that box I dragged in that's *actually* interesting?"

Tristan considered this question. As a local historian and archivist for the Council he knew that to everyday folk he came across as a little bit odd. Old bits of yellowing paper excited him. He could spend days happily squinting through small-print news articles that described the most mundane provincial transactions. Ancient recipes, nineteenth century farming bills and village death registers were like juicy celebrity gossip to Tristan: irresistible.

"Yes."

"Okay, so how can I help? I'm no historian, lad."

Tristan shifted his weight on the worn carpet tiles. "Maybe not, but you're an expert on Seatown. You're on our streets twenty-four-seven; nowt gets past you."

"So you want to pick my brain?" Ernie asked. "It's unclean, mind. Not for the faint of heart."

"I just want your thoughts on these meeting minutes," Tristan said, extracting a handful of yellowing sheets from the folder. Most of them had crinkled edges and bore faint charcoal-coloured smudges, as well as the whiff of trout. "They date from the seventeen sixties and they look like they've been in a fire. I'm thinking what happened was..."

"A fire destroyed the Seatown Customs House," Ernie interrupted.

"Yeah, I was going to say that," Tristan bristled. "In 1771."

"That's right, lad. Back when Stan Tweddle were in nappies," Ernie chuckled. "Let's have a look, then. Do we not need to be wearing white gloves?"

"We're not handling Samuel Pepys' diary, Ernie. And did you forget you found them in a skip?"

"Right enough."

Tristan fanned the pages onto the floor in front of them. "They're very faded but I think they're recording a public meeting. There's a lot of talk about smugglers, criminal activity and outrage. But in eighteenth century English."

Ernie nodded. "No need to read it out loud, Trit, otherwise I'll go cross-eyed."

"Does any of this sound familiar to you, Ernie?"

The older man stretched his arms over his head; Tristan winced as the smell of Seatown harbour wafted over him. "There've been whispers of pirate activity for many a year."

While Ernie considered the criminal nature of his beloved hometown, Tristan subtly shifted back a few inches, grateful for a few breaths of fresh air. *Between the fish and chips, the fishy paper and Ernie's armpits, Janet will pass out when she walks in here tomorrow.*

"Is that right?" Tristan asked him. "Do I *not* know because I'm an off-comer?" *I might be Cumbrian but I'm not a Seatownian.*

"Well, lad, not everything's written down in books," Ernie started. "Seatown's a proud community. But not so much nowadays, what with all the cheap pints and smart kids like Courtney not being able to work. We don't talk much about the darker side of our history. Things are rough enough without bringing that all up. More grist for the newspapers and TV crews, eh?

Tristan stood up, not without some difficulty. "I think you may have had a point about eating in the kitchen," he groaned. "I'm not as fit as I thought. Why don't we go downstairs with this lot and I make us both a cuppa? Maybe a biccie or two?"

Below them came a thump and a clatter.

Chapter Thirteen

Two black shadows, one tall and thin, the other not, lingered by the library door.

"Good idea and all coming a bit later, but what if the police spot us?" asked the tall, thin one, his pale face peering out into the quiet street.

"Police? What police?" mocked the other one as he stuffed a key into the main door lock. "I know this key works Ian, so we're going in. I need to find summat that'll shut this dump down *and* those documents they were wittering on about."

Ian jumped from foot to foot, uneasy with his role as unwitting sidekick. "What'll we say if someone does stop us?"

"'*Council business*' has always worked in the past," Norman spat. "No reason why it shouldn't now. People know better than to ask questions."

"Hmmm."

"Don't 'hmmm' me, lad. Have you got that alarm code handy?"

Ian pulled a damp piece of paper from his jacket pocket. "Don't ask me how I got this," he joked. "Thelma had me in the stationery cupboard, right up against…"

"I don't care, Ian. Just get ready to disable it in two seconds."

Following a slew of profanities the lock clicked open and the men stumbled into the cold, hard sound of silence. Norman shone the beam of his phone torch onto the 'Cumbria Security' keypad: not a flashing light in sight.

"They must have forgotten to set the alarm?" Ian suggested, easing past Councillor Roach to rest against a revolving bookcase of children's books. "It only covers the ground floor, anyway. The upstair's sensor has been broken for months."

Norman swung around, aiming the torch at Ian's eyes. "No, you pillock, there are people here. Can't you smell that?"

"Smell what?" Ian yelped, as the rotating bookcase propelled him onto a small pile of children's playing blocks.

Above them came the sound of footsteps.

Norman shoved his phone back in his pocket and pulled open the door. "You bloody idiot!"

Scrambling to his feet, Ian tried and failed to grab a hold of the twirling bookcase. "For God's sake, Norman!"

From the discomfort of the children's reading section, two things occured to Ian. One, the disappearing shadow of Councillor Norman Roach confirmed that he had been left behind. And two, his sense of smell had finally caught up with him. *Is that cod or haddock?*

Two sets of feet thundered down the stairs.

Ian stood up and braced himself against the 'Young Adult' reading section.

Two murmuring voices travelled towards him.

"Did you lock the door?"

"Shush, Ernie."

He watched Tristan Pear approach, with Ernie Noble shuffling at the rear.

"It's a bit late for Suzanne Collins, isn't it?" Tristan joked. "Who are you?"

Ian removed a business card from his wallet and handed it to Tristan. "Ian Nicholson, facilities management."

"And why are you here, Ian Nicholson?"

"Council business...?"

Ernie studied Ian, then swept his eyes over the floor. "What's this?" he asked, bending down to pick up a piece of crumpled paper. "Urgh. Bit damp, eh?"

Tristan looked over Ernie's shoulder. "That's our alarm code. Why have you got our alarm code, Ian? Hardly security conscious, is it?"

Ian's hands dripped with sweat. "Well, eh, I'm doing a security spot check, you see. And, eh, you've breached Council regulations by keeping your facility open after hours without notifying US." With his returning confidence came a wavering increase in volume.

"Was someone else with you?" Tristan asked. "We heard voices."

Ian laughed. "I was, um, on the phone. Letting Thelma know I'd arrived. She's our team leader."

"Your arse," Ernie muttered.

"Well, why are *you* both here?" Ian asked them. "And you, Mr. Noble. Is this not your night for a bit of harbour watching?"

Ernie started towards him. "What do you know about my comings and goings? Have we met?"

Ian didn't try to correct the man; he knew a dangerous member of the public when he came across one.

Tristan moved in front of Ernie. "We're doing some research, Ian…,"

"Mr. Nicholson."

"…and we weren't expecting a security check, whatever that's supposed to be. So, maybe go and find your friend and ask if they can offer a better explanation."

Ernie squeezed himself in between the two men and sniffed the air. "That's *Acqua Di Gio* for men. And not the market knock-off. I know who wears that," he whispered in Ian's ear.

"What on earth are you talking about?" Ian accused, jumping out of Ernie's way. "This is my aftershave; not that you'd know anything about good hygiene."

Tristan shuffled Ian out onto the street. "Ian. Mr. Nicholson. Ernie and I have some work to continue with."

"Aye, tell Norman Cockroach that I'm on to him," Ernie roared, digging Tristan with his elbow.

"There'll be repercussions," Ian spat, smoothing his hair with trembling hands. "That old tramp threatened me for a start. And you, Mr. Pear, wouldn't allow us access to the building. You could be hiding something for all we know."

"Us? We? You're getting your pronouns mixed up."

Ernie thrust his hand towards Ian, the piece of paper dangling between his fingers. "Don't forget your sweaty alarm code, buster."

Tristan grabbed and pocketed it. "We'll keep that, Ernie."

***

Norman was trying to enjoy a steaming hot doner kebab. On his lap lay a grease-soaked copy of that week's Seatown Chronicle, the front page headline accusing Council members of fraud, in large black type.

Thick, creamy sauce dripped onto the ink, smearing it into a garlicky paste.

His phone trilled.

"I'm eating, love," he said, noticing that his device was now coated in mayonnaise.

"Whatever, dad. I need you to order in salon equipment for me, and store it somewhere too. I'll send you an email."

"Janine, the site's not ready yet. We need to have patience!"

"My clients can't wait, dad! They need lip fillers and they need them in an aesthetically pleasing, stark-white clinic. Seatown's full of nasty old buildings. They're filthy. I want a new building."

Norman swallowed a chunk of donner meat. "Clinic? Is it not a salon?"

Call ended.

Through his rear view mirror Norman registered a fast approaching tall, thin shadow.

"Let me in!" it squawked, pulling at the passenger door handle.

The window lowered a few inches forcing takeaway fumes into the fresh night air. "Keep it down, lad. What happened?"

"What happened?" Ian shouted towards the shape within. "We got rumbled, is what happened!

Norman wiped his glistening chin with a handful of paper napkins. "What do you mean, 'we'? I'm here in my car, Ian."

Ian stepped back, shaking his head. "We're done, NORMAN."

Norman pushed a plump finger through the window gap. "You'll never be more than a tiny fish in a shallow puddle, Ian. Run along, now. I'll get what *I* need and *you'll* see the dole queue.

Chapter Fourteen

The following Monday morning...

"So, Mr. Tweddle, you're telling us that Ernie Noble *isn't* to blame for the library closing?" Gavin McKenna asked, as he crunched on a chewed up biro. Rain lashed off the small window by his desk.

"That's right, lad," Stan shouted down the phone. "Just as well you didn't print my letter about his urination, eh? Can I, um, ask why you didn't?" Stan fully expected the journalist to spew excuses. After all, those in power were forced to protect each other.

"We would have been at risk of libel, sir. Spurious claims against members of the public are a path to an expensive lawsuit."

Stan hadn't thought of that. "Oh, right enough."

Gavin decided to take a punt. "So, Mr. Tweddle, you're a man in the know. Have you any ideas why the library might be closing? Libraries aren't exactly sexy news."

That surprised Stan; he assumed these bodies met in remote basements to make important decisions. "I'm not sure I should tell you that, Gavin. And call me Stan, won't you? Your letters page would be a dry desert if it wasn't for me."

Gavin was slightly taken aback by this rare show of self-awareness. Stan was a joke in the office but he filled column space. "Stan, where would we be without local knowledge like yours?"

Stan knew a lickspittle when he heard one breathing down the phone. "Hold on a minute, Gavin. Libraries aren't sexy but bin collections are?"

"Elections rest on waste management, Stan, not book borrowing."

"Well, that's not right," Stan snipped. Using words like 'sexy' made his insides blush.

"It's not, but we've got to sell papers," Gavin whispered into the phone, "otherwise I'll end up selling ad space in a free mag and I can't let that happen, Stan. Ever."

"Sales is an honest living, lad," Stan bristled. "It's what I did for forty years."

"Really? I took you more for an inspector of some sort."

"No, ladies cosmetics. Anyway, the library. It's not busy enough, it's going to close and it's your public duty to help."

Gavin scribbled in his notebook. "There *are* a quiet couple of weeks coming up, bar any surprise fires, deaths or lay-offs. Who should I speak to in the library? It's Jeanette, isn't it?"

"Janet, lad. You should talk to Janet. Why don't you call in? But avoid Bev Rogers. And that Courtney Harrison one."

"Um, alright. I'll maybe call in some day before lunch. There's a Greggs next door, right?"

"No, a proper bakery. 'The La'al Teacake.'"

Gavin was a little disappointed. "Okay, Stan, I'll do it for my best informa...source."

Stan knew better than to bite; his library computer was more important. "And Ernie Noble."

"What?"

"Avoid Ernie Noble."

"Bu-bye, Stan," Gavin said, dropping the phone onto his desk.

***

"Pam?"

A red-haired woman in a pale blue trouser suit looked up from her chicken salad. "What's up, Gav?"

The journalist sauntered over to his editor's desk. "I've just been talking to Stan the Snitch."

Pam stabbed a crouton with her fork. "What's he twining about now?"

Pam had final say on features. Gavin knew she was struggling to fill space and thought the library story might garner some tasty soundbites from the great and the good of Seatown. "He says the library might close."

"Well, yeah. The land's worth a fortune, isn't it?"

Gavin blinked. "What? He didn't mention that!"

"Gavin McKenna not in the loop? Considering you spend most nights eavesdropping at the 'Drunken Sailor', I'm shocked," Pam joked, wiping mayonnaise from her chin with the back of her hand.

"Well, where have *you* been eavesdropping?" he asked, stroppily kicking the paper recycling bin by her desk. To his disgust Pam pulled a tissue from her bag, blew her nose and chucked it in it.

"Can't reveal my source, chuck. But it's not to be printed. Do you hear me?"

"Why not? It would be a great story. Well, a decent story, anyway. It's no, 'fly-tipped medical waste,' or, 'arming the local constabulary,' but it might sell."

Pam eye-balled him. "Because I want to keep my job, that's why not."

***

A local television news story on dog mess drew Stan's attention away from the cordless phone in his hand.

After some satisfying tutting at the television he returned his attention to the phone, but before he could end the call, the handset dispensed a ghostly whisper.

What's that? He placed the handset back to his ear and listened to Gavin call him Stan the Snitch.

And he heard more.

Chapter Fifteen

The same day…

With a heavy head and a churning stomach, Janet shook her dripping umbrella onto the wet street and opened the library doors.

Her weekend had been full of Maltesers and wine. She usually ate poor quality chocolate and drank bottom-shelf grape juice when she was happy and when she was sad. That weekend she'd indulged because she was something in between: cautiously hopeful.

Adam, her long-term, extremely casual boyfriend, supplied the goodies and, when he hadn't been playing Fantasy Football on his phone, a listening ear. Adam was a joiner and they'd met when he'd fitted her kitchen ten years previously. The very definition of laid-back, Adam's biggest commitment in life had been the purchase of a doer-upper terraced house on Lupin's street, the rent from which provided him with a steady trickle of beer money. To his credit, he walked Spark Pug without complaining about it being a 'girlie dog'.

Saturday had gotten off to a breezy and slightly hungover start with a fell ramble that Adam promised would be easy on the quadriceps.

After fifteen strenuous minutes Janet had lost the power of speech and was starting to seriously consider if this had been Adam's primary intention after a long night spent debating the future of the library.

As the wine bottles had emptied, the pair had boozily swung between waging all out war against Council officials to reinstating pirate lawlessness in Seatown and squatting in the library.

A mutual craving for fish and chips saw the pair tumble back down with only minimal knee strain. A pleasant supper at the harbour ended with Adam heading home to Match of the Day and Janet to her busy thoughts.

***

Janet and Lupin had scheduled a ten o'clock meeting with Reverend Nixon to discuss extending the men's mental health programme, the waiting list of which was running into double figures.

Watching Lupin come into work with her head down broke Janet's heart. Her peculiar next-in-command had proved herself to be loyal and hard-working with a passion for books and community. She was the ideal shipmate. Yet her recent drop in mood clung to the library like a wet chill.

"Hi, love. Did you have a good weekend?"

Lupin dragged herself to the back of the reception desk and dropped into a chair. "Oh, it was lovely,

Janet. Bert threw me the sign of the cross every time I left the house and my tea leaves reminded me that I can't escape my past."

"Lup, you can't dwell on history. Every family has a dark side; some are just better at hiding it than others."

"Exactly, Janet. We were doing a right good job of hiding it until Ernie threw that manky box of history at us."

Before Janet could offer Lupin a soothing cup of tea, a damp Tristan stormed in.

"Ladies, I held off texting you all weekend just so I could have the pleasure of telling you this in person."

Lupin pulled a face. "Tristan, can you not call us 'ladies'?"

Janet bit her lip.

"Women, I've got scandal!" Tristan exclaimed, raising his eyebrows at Lupin. "Happy, Lup?"

Janet herded both of them into the kitchen. "Let's do this somewhere more private, in case Violet and crew burst in."

"Us being in the kitchen won't stop her," Lupin said.

"True, but by the look on Tristan's face I get the feeling we're going to need tea."

Janet filled the kettle, Lupin rinsed some cups and Tristan drummed his fingers on the kitchen table.

"I'm losing momentum here," he complained.

"Maybe we should wait for Pete," Lupin suggested, drying the mugs with a dirty tea towel.

Janet sighed. "Get on with it, Tristan, before you wet yourself. As long as you don't mind me having my back to you."

"Ernie and I were here on Friday night, right? We were making some progress with *ye olde* documents when we heard a racket."

Janet poured boiling water into the mugs, disappointed that she couldn't turn around in shock. "What? Who was it? Was it that gang of twelve year olds that call themselves the Market Place Posse? I'll have their guts for garters, the little thugs."

Lupin sat down beside Tristan. "So, who was it?"

"Some prat called Ian Nicholson literally fell into the young adult section. He claimed he was from the Council and was here to carry out a 'security check'."

"I can't believe you made air quotation marks, Tristan," Lupin scoffed.

"What's got into you, Lup? You not been meditating?"

Janet slammed three cups of tea onto the table. "I know it's a wet Monday morning but can we please lose the mardy-arseness and get to the matter at hand".

Tristan whispered into Lupin's ear, "She's hungover."

"For that, Mr. Pear, you're not getting a biscuit," Janet said, slapping his hand.

"Sorry, I'll behave for a custard cream. Anyway, Ian, whoever he is, had very obviously not been acting alone because we heard two voices. And he had our security code on a piece of paper."

Enthralled, Lupin stared at Tristan as she gulped her tea. "So, who was he with?"

"Hold that thought, Lupin," Janet asked, turning to Tristan. "Did you leave the front door open?"

"No! And even if I had, when was the last time anyone stole a library book, Janet?"

"Eh, Jenny Jessop nicked our whole Bill Bryson stock two years ago?"

"To get back to my fascinating story," Tristan continued. "Ernie smelled aftershave."

Janet clapped her hands. "There are only about five thousand men of aftershave-wearing age in Seatown, so that narrows it down a bit."

"It was Councillor Roach's aftershave," Tristan deadpanned.

"That bas - "

The door opened to reveal a visibly disappointed Pete. "Oh, you've already made the tea."

Chapter Sixteen

Pete quickly recovered from his tea disappointment to set up Meeting Room two for 'Ur Future Now,' a twelve-week employability programme for eighteen to twenty-five year olds living in and around Seatown.

As he struggled to disentangle a tower of stackable chairs, a shockingly early Courtney crept up behind him and flicked him on the ear.

"Ow!" he yelped, brandishing a metal-framed chair at his attacker.

Courtney leapt back with a nervous giggle, grateful that Pete hadn't broken her nose and expelled a full face of complicated contouring.

"I thought you'd have heard me, Pete!" she wailed.

Pete pointed to her feet. "You're wearing trainers, for God's sake! I could have seriously hurt you."

"No offence, Pete but you wouldn't have."

Pete shrugged. "We'll agree to disagree."

"You're so sensible, Pete," she said, inching forward to flick his other ear but changing her mind at the last second. "So, do you think we should organise a big event?"

"What for?" he asked, mentally calculating how many seats he'd need to set out.

"I dunno," she said, scuffing the carpet tiles with her trainer. "Something to help the library."

Pete arranged the chairs in a neat semi-circle. "Have you any ideas?"

"Not really, that's why I thought we could work together on it, like."

"I think we should do something funny. Like an eating contest." *Please say sausage rolls, please say sausage rolls.*

She nodded her agreement. "As long as Ernie doesn't take part, or I'll blow this place up with him in it."

"Aye, alright. Maybe I'll schedule a planning meeting, eh?"

"Really? Like here? Or, at the pub?" Courtney beamed, struggling to remain cool.

"Wherever. We'll need to sort the logistics." *Good lad, that's a big word.*

"Great, text me the details. Or whatever." *He said logistics.*

At this point Janet swooped in, immediately scalded by the heat radiating off both of their faces.

"Have I interrupted anything, young people?"

"Em, no," Pete said, needlessly re-adjusting his chairs. "Just talking about sausage rolls."

Courtney's brow was a deep trench. "You what?"

Janet didn't waste time asking for an explanation. "Courtney, why don't you skip off this class and come to our meeting with Reverend Nixon?"

"But then I'll miss this one. We're doing job search this week and I'm dead good at that."

"Don't worry," Janet soothed. "It won't take long, you'll not miss much."

"Do you want me to make the Rev a cuppa tea?" she asked, pointing at Pete. "Cos that's his job."

"No lass, we need your help."

***

Two minutes before ten o'clock, Reverend Nixon ducked into the library and loped towards the signing-in book. It took seven steps.

Lupin greeted him from behind the front desk. "Morning Reverend, has it dried up out there?

Other than her best-forgotten rendezvous with a freshly graduated vicar, men of the cloth didn't warm to Lupin. Most introductions would go as follows: the aged vicar would slyly size up her namaste tattoo, 'evil eye' pendant and nose ring, sniff, then limply shake her hand.

But thankfully, Reverend Nixon was the kind of man to blithely accept anyone as a friend, his big personality only ever welcoming, never judging.

"Morning Lupin!" he beamed. "I swore I saw a bit of blue sky over the water, so maybe it'll fair up soon. How are you?"

"I'm very well, thanks. And you?"

Reverend Nixon shrugged. "All I'll say is this: a shrinking congregation and a growing maintenance bill can drive a man to sherry."

"We know how you feel, Rev. Only with us, it's tequila. And blue cocktails."

"Oh, Lupin," he commiserated, casting his eye over the ground floor. "Are you having a touch of trouble?"

"You could say that, vicar," Janet revealed, rounding the corner to shake his hand.

***

Once settled around the room's least wonky table, Pete having just safely settled a tray of tea, coffee and biscuits onto its scratched surface, Courtney started to ponder what she had done wrong.

She'd once called the Reverend Nixon, 'Knicks Off', but she was nearly certain it had never got back to him as he'd only ever been nice to her. Nervous, maybe, but always friendly, though he did question her employment status more than she'd have liked.

"Did you want me to take the minutes, Janet?" she asked, pulling on the drawstring of her pink hoodie. "It's just, I'm not sure what that means. Do I time how long the meeting will last?"

Janet leaned over and patted Courtney's hand. "Sorry love, I should have explained myself but it's been one of those days."

"And it's only eleven o'clock," Lupin moaned.

Ignoring Lupin's dark mood, Janet continued. "The Reverend is here to talk about expanding his Men's Mental Health programme, Court. But he doesn't know about our current predicament."

"You mean Ernie's dribbles?" she asked. "Or Stan Tweddle sending hate mail to the Women's Institute? What have I got to do with those? I'm no snitch."

Lupin's raised eyebrows grazed the damp ceiling tile above her head. "Well, now…"

Janet shot Lupin a look. "No Courtney, he doesn't know about our impending closure."

Until now the Reverend had been pouring tea and coffee, biting his tongue to the extent that he could taste blood. But his rising giggle soon came to an abrupt halt. "You're closing? We can't allow that!"

"Who's we?" Courtney asked."You mean God? Can you put a good word in for me? Don't mention Ernie. Like, at all."

"No Courtney, I meant the Diocese," he replied, registering the disappointment in her face. "But God won't be pleased either."

Janet cleared her throat. "Reverend, your men's programme is really popular. I'll admit, I thought you'd have little to no chance of convincing Seatown blokes to come here and talk about their feelings. You know, in front of people. But they have. And there are loads more waiting for a spot."

To Lupin's delight Reverend Nixon put his hands together, as if in prayer. *He's such a vicar. Bless.*

"It has been a tremendous success, Janet. And in no small part to your wonderful communications."

"She has literally taken men by the scruff of the neck and pulled them in off the street to sign up," Courtney exclaimed.

Janet shook her head. "That's not quite true, Courtney."

"Whatever your methods," he said, "they've really helped. But now I hear this news and I'm speechless!"

"Well, get ready to take a vow of silence, Rev," Lupin began. "Because we've only been given three piddly months to increase our numbers and I can't imagine how we're going to pull it off."

Janet circumvented Courtney's imminent snigger with a wrap to the ankle from her heavy duty black suede boot. *Why did I bring her in here, again?*

"Ow!"

"Courtney, tell the Reverend Nixon what you've been doing in the library this past year."

"I'll just check my resumé," she said, puffing out her cheeks and pulling her phone from her jeans pocket "That's a C.V., Rev."

The vicar nodded kindly.

"Right," she said, scrolling through the online document. "So, basically, I've done loads of courses through the library's community learning programme. They've helped me get some decent work, but then I get laid off. Not my fault, mind. Places are just closing all the time, eh?"

"What kind of courses?" the man inquired. "Employability programmes and the like?"

"Yeah. Tons of those. For people like me."

Lupin and Janet exchanged a glance.

"People like you, Courtney?" the Reverend frowned. "What do you mean?"

"You know, people with no skills or prospects," she stated. "I was rubbish in school and Mam said she needed me at home to put nana on the toilet."

Janet cleared her throat. "Reverend Nixon, people like Courtney, and your men, rely on this library. Community centres are closing all the time and the local college won't offer places to youngsters with a poor educational record."

"We're running out of space," Lupin confirmed.

"Indeed, indeed," said the Reverend, frowning. "Our church hall is in such a state. The roof is full of holes and well, we've not got the money..."

"What a mess, eh?" Courtney chuckled. "This place is closing, the church hall's full of rain water and college thinks I'm a chav."

The Reverend Nixon reached for the teapot and poured himself a fresh cup of tea. "Anyone else?"

All three nodded.

"These meetings are thirsty work," Courtney said, looking around the room with her mouth open. "I've never been in a meeting before. Apart from in the job centre, like."

After topping up everyone's tea the Reverend returned to his seat and pulled a notebook and pen from his jacket pocket.

"Now then, let's make a plan."

Courtney held up her hand. "High five, vicar. Who's going to say no to you, eh?"

The Reverend lightly tapped her open palm. "We'll see, Courtney, we'll see."

Quietly thrilled, Janet tapped the tube of *Pink Desire* that lay snug in her trouser pocket. Following a long moment of deliberation she concluded that it would be inappropriate to apply lippy in front of a man of God.

Chapter Seventeen

The combined Craft, Creative Writing and Save our Library club assembled in Violet's comfortable home for its first official meeting.

The super group was born following Helen's refusal to participate in three separate Whatsapp groups. She claimed the endless notifications disturbed her thrice-daily tai chi.

Violet secretly agreed with Helen; Tina had no place posting line dancing clips on all three groups. The main aim of the club was the library campaign, not drunk pensioners tripping over each other to the strains of Achy Breaky Heart. There was a time and place for hunky, chunky country and western singers and this wasn't it.

"Come in, Ernie. You can, er, keep your shoes on if you like," Violet offered as the man slunk over her doorstep, bearing a flimsy plastic bag containing what looked like loose jammy dodgers.

Ernie's laceless brogues slipped straight off to reveal immaculate silk socks in a fetching shade of mauve. "Surprised, aren't you, Vi?"

Violet was speechless. Accepting the bag of biscuits with a level of grace that pained her she pointed him in the direction of the good room. From the hallway Ernie clocked Royal Doulton and heavy ruched curtains.

He found Helen, Malcolm and Tina squashed together on the Chesterfield, Malcolm stuck squarely in the middle and looking very pleased with himself.

"Morning ladies. Where should I park my dainty behind?"

Tina pointed to a highly polished mahogany dining set. "None of us wanted to sit on the armchairs. You know what Vi's like."

"Aye, lass, I do," he responded, before settling himself onto a royal blue Parker Knoll armchair. "The Pit should get some of these; it's like sitting on a big marshmallow."

The tut-tutting could be heard in Northumberland.

While Violet busied herself with meringues in the kitchen, Agatha C introduced herself to the Chesterfield occupants by weaving around each of their legs.

"You alright there, Helen?" Ernie asked.

"Perfectly fine, Ernie," she replied, plucking dog hair from her trouser legs with manicured fingers. "It's just that these linen pants cost a lot of money and it's the first time I've put them on."

"Dogs will do that, lass. She's just trying to make friends, aren't you petal?" he said, reaching forward to tickle the pup's pink belly.

"Is Agatha behaving herself?" Violet shouted from the kitchen.

"Yes, Vi," Malcolm piped up. "She's showing us her belly."

Malcolm crawled onto the floor beside her. "Aren't you a lovely girl? Yes, you are!"

"I never took Malcolm for a dog lover," Tina gasped, looking sideways at Helen. "He's so particular about his clothes."

"My grandad had a lovely little Yorkshire terrier called Scamp," he explained, lying prostrate on the floor by his new best friend. "I was the only person in the house he wouldn't wee on. He loved me."

***

John was loitering by the back door, trowel in hand, desperate to be allowed back into the garden, his green and tranquil safe space.

"John," Violet hissed, amidst the steam of a boiling kettle. "Take off your wellies and check where Ernie's sitting. But don't let them see you! I could have sworn I heard the Parker Knoll creaking."

Violet's husband kicked off his wellies and padded towards the living room on thick, woollen socks, blades of grass drifting gently onto the mock oak floorboards.

He slunk back to his wife. "He's on the PK. What should I do?"

"The damage is done," she sighed, chucking mini Eton mess desserts onto the Portmeirion. "Best leave him be."

"Can I get back to my herbaceous borders, petal?"

Grabbing a tin of squirty cream from the countertop Violet dispensed a tiny little blob on the end of her husband's nose and kissed it off. "Yes, Mellors, get back to tending my garden."

_____ *** _____

"Ernie Noble, you have a knack for getting the best seat in the house," Violet proclaimed, pushing a loaded hostess trolley into the living room.

A wayward wheel caught on the fringes of her Turkish rug, tipping a miniature milk jug onto a plate of oven-fresh fruit scones. "Oh, bugger."

"You'd be disappointed if I didn't park myself on the throne, lass," he retorted. "And I knew Malcolm were gagging for a Helen and Tina sandwich."

While Malcolm looked like the cat that got the cream, Tina and Helen looked like they'd stepped in cat sick.

"Violet, let me help you clear up," Tina offered, pushing herself off the sofa.

149

"It's quite alright," Violet protested, waving the woman away. "I'll mop it up. Can't be helped when you've got an authentic Turkish rug. You know how it is."

"We'd avoid further mishaps if there were fewer bodies on the carpet," Helen said, shooting daggers at an oblivious Malcolm. "Eh, Doctor Doolittle?"

"Aye, Doctor Doo-bugger-all," Ernie chimed in, reaching down to pet Agatha C.

"That's my hair!" Malcolm yelped, popping up from the side of the Parker Knoll.

"Urgh, I thought I could feel brylcreem on my fingers."

Violet started pouring the tea. "Ernie, go and wash your hands."

"I will if you keep an eye on my seat."

"It's like being at school," Tina said, shaking her head.

Ernie looked puzzled. "Why, were you held back, Tina?"

After a messy tea that saw Violet sweep up meringue crumbs at least half dozen times, she assembled a desktop flip chart onto the highly polished surface of her dining table.

"Very fancy," Malcolm said, impressed. "Did you take that from the library?"

"I did not! I bought it…"

"…at the Thursday market," Helen deadpanned.

"Excuse me, but I bought it from Simpson's Stationery on Railway Street."

"I can't believe that place is still open, what with Amazon taking over the world," Tina said. "You know, my son bought a stapler for ninety pence from Amazon. That can't be right."

Ignoring them, Violet rummaged through her pencil case for two markers.

"Those are definitely from the library," Ernie laughed.

Violet smirked. "Maybe."

"Right, enough chit chat," she continued. "We need to get down to the business of saving our library."

"Well, I've been thinking," Ernie began, sitting forward on his chair. "I get all my best ideas at night, because I don't sleep much. Anyway, it were four in the morning and I was catching up on Strictly when it came to me. How about we…"

"Don't!" Violet shouted, waving her marker at him. "We're not robbing or burning anything."

Ernie grabbed a lace antimacassar from the arm of the Parker Knoll and blew his nose into it. "I'm not stupid, Violet."

Stupefied, the club watched Ernie ball up the antimacassar and stuff it into his pocket.

Helen blessed herself. "Did he just...?"

"Anyway, we should hold an awareness-raising tea dance at Malcolm's old folks home. I know they've got a big old ballroom that sits empty most of the time, apart from the odd game of armchair boccia, which they're terrible at."

There was a moment's silence.

Ernie continued. "Malcolm can butter the manager up. She'll go for it because she fancies him. We can all help out. Stan will get the papers involved. Pete and Courtney can pour the tea. "

Violet dropped her marker. "I haven't written a word yet."

"Louise fancies me?" Malcolm asked, eyes like saucers.

Tina looked confused. "But how will a tea dance keep the library open?"

"Well, lass," Ernie continued, settling into the armchair. "People love a bit of a do, right? While they're dancing and swigging tea we can talk to 'em about our Pit. The women can suck up to the big wigs and we can have a nice photo display of all the stupid events the Pit has held over the years. Maybe gerra few young 'uns to talk about those training courses for dossers. Don't ask Courtney though, otherwise they'll lock the doors shut and throw away the key."

"Sounds like you've got it all planned," Violet sniffed.

"Get your marker, Vi and make some bullet holes," Ernie commanded. "We've got to make a plan."

"Bullet points," Helen huffed.

Chapter Eighteen

Sail masts rattled as the wind hurtled through them, the ensuing whistle casting an eerie cloak over the harbour.

"Slow down, you show off," Hazel gasped, clasping a hand to her chest.

Maeve's bright yellow trainers hammered ahead of her on the rough harbour path.

"Oh my God, I can't keep up," Hazel laughed, squinting into the bright, cloudless sky. "Can we have a break? Please!"

Cackling gulls fought over scattered chips by the harbour memorial.

Maeve plonked down onto a bench in surrender. "You know we may as well quit here every week. No point aiming for further when this seat has your bum print on it."

"You cheeky mare," Hazel puffed, easing herself onto the cold wooden slats with a groan. "You know walking is just as good for us as running."

"You call that effort running?" Maeve teased, giving her friend a nudge.

They looked out towards the horizon, quietly appreciating the soothing swell of the sea.

Hazel turned to her friend. "So, what's next, doll?"

"You mean other than planting a bomb under Norman's desk?"

"Yeah."

Maeve picked at a stray thread on her leggings. "It might be time to start dusting those top shelves."

"The 'Drunken Sailor' won't know what hit it."

Chapter Nineteen

Normally, Tristan liked to spend his evenings poring over vintage travel brochures, dreaming of old-fashioned travel to far-flung places where you could smoke cigars on the plane and wear speedos on the beach, unironically.

But tonight every surface in his small, town-centre flat was buried under sheets of old paper that smelt like a neglected county museum.

"What is it, Tristan? We're on the last episode of Stranger Things!" bawled a disembodied voice.

With a hot mug of coffee in one hand and a Tunnock's teacake in the other, Tristan loomed over the aged documents, mobile phone perched on the threadbare arm of his favourite, and only, armchair.

"Alright, keep your helmet hair on," he joked.

"You're getting on my last nerve, laddo. Adam's threatening to put the footie on if you don't hurry up."

Tristan rolled his eyes. "He wouldn't dare."

"Aye, I would!" Adam shouted. "Get a move on, anorak."

"I've spent days looking through Ernie's documents and my hands are in shreds from washing because this paper is diseased. Anyway, I think there's something here."

"Like what?" Janet asked, the glug of pouring wine reverberating around Tristan's living room. "Don't keep us in suspenders, we've got nineteen eighties kids to cheer on."

Tristan swiped a sheet from the lid of his fish tank. "Forget the nineteen eighties. A covenant was drawn up in seventeen hundred and summat to protect the Madeleine Pit library from closure for ever and ever, amen."

"Flipping heck," Janet spluttered. "Fetch that paper in tomorrow, before…"

"…it finds its way into Norman's shredder. Yeah, I'm way ahead of you."

***

Breaststroke was her least favourite. She was terrified of morphing into one of those twice-weekly swimmers that refused to get their hair wet. The breaststroke devotees with perfect makeup harnessed in upholstered Marks and Spencer costumes. Scaffolding for swimming.

Breaststroke was her least favourite for those reasons. But she enjoyed gliding through the water like an otter and the chlorine-to-cavities ratio was more favourable than front crawl.

The local leisure centre was recently refurbished, boasting additional diving boards for teenage show-offs, a hot drinks machine for waiting parents and an indoor bowls room for steady-armed men and women of pension age.

Every time Lupin rounded the street corner she was surprised to find the centre still open. Shivering damp-haired kids grasping cans of cold pop would rush past her; gangs of chattering old gents would lumber by, cradling their lucky bowling balls. It was a place of constant activity. Muscled young gym assistants would take block bookings from five-a-side teams then get called away to rescue lost shuttlecocks.

And all the while the mingling scent of chemicals and rubber clung to every available surface.

_____ *** _____

This was the worst part. The desperate rush from warm water, to dribbling shower, to boiling, cramped changing room. Extra points if you could avoid adopting other people's shedded hair as a pool pet. Lupin peeled off a long, blonde tendril from her calf and wiped it against the cubicle wall. *When I win the lottery I'll build myself a heated, indoor pool. So, I'd better start doing the lottery.*

As she focused on drying herself off, Lupin overheard raised voices in the double cubicle next door. It was impossible not to eavesdrop, not when her boss's name was suddenly barked into the thick, humid air.

"That Janet one thinks she owns the Pit. Marching about with her hair and her lipstick. She's a throwback to a golden age that never happened, I'm telling you."

There followed a moment's huffing and puffing. "Amanda, love, can you not talk about work? Here, help me pull this cossie up. It's so wet in here, everything's sticking."

"Stick your belly in, mum! Alright, there you go. Is that a new suit?"

"Aye, M&S. Got a lovely ruched tummy panel, doesn't it?"

"Hmmm. Anyway, if Norman has anything to do with it he'll have the library demolished."

"But why, love? Where would I get my Grishams if the Mad Pit's closed?

"Did you not read those romances I got you for your birthday?"

"Naw love, too soppy for me. I need fit, young lawyers running around the big city."

The shared cubicle wall trembled.

"Ow! What are you doing, mum? Is that mascara?"

"It's waterproof. I can't go in there bare-faced. Did you know Jeanie Barwell gets her hair done just to come to the ladies' swim?"

"There's me worrying about Norman Roach buying up half of Seatown when my seventy-six year-old mother is wearing makeup to the pool."

"Pet, Janet's a good soul. So what if she's got hair like Maggie Thatcher?"

_____ *** _____

Lupin left the leisure centre feeling damper than when she'd gone in.

She started to angry walk. Angry walking was bad for the chakras but good for drying wet hair.

If I could astral project into Norman Cockroach's filing cabinet, we'd be home and dry.

Her soggy ears were blasted by the cold, night air.

I really wish I was home and dry.

Chapter Twenty

"It's Hormonal Hour, better open the windows for the sweating ladies," Stan jeered, waving at a poster for the local menopause support group. He picked up the Seatown Chronicle, frowned and replaced it on the foyer table.

Ernie scowled into his 'La'al Teacake' flat white. "What's up, Mr. Avon? Disappointed you've not made the headlines this week?"

"Not at all. Look at the state of you, man. When's the last time your face saw soap?"

"The last time you got your leg over, which would have been nineteen sixty-eight, or thereabouts."

Pete stood by Autobiographies and watched the two men. *Will I end up like those two?*

As he scanned the room he clocked Courtney walking towards her Level 2 Cyber Security course flanked by two young men wearing baseball caps and rapt expressions.

Pete knew he had to do something really difficult.

Edging along a row of Freddie Flintoff biographies he faked a sneeze. It was loud and obnoxious.

"Is that Donald Duck getting molested?" baseball hat wearer number one wheezed into Courtney's ear.

His mate groaned, gutted at having lost a golden opportunity to impress the woman of his cyber security class daydreams.

Courtney tenderly touched Pete's hand, then thought better of it and bounced back onto the heels of her trainers. "You alright? It's not catching, is it?"

"Um." *She touched my hand.*

"You're not dying, then?" *I touched his hand.*

"It's just dust. Listen, are you free tomorrow night?"

Convinced he could see her heart beating, Courtney zipped up her jacket. "I'll tell Maeve you said that. What for?"

"Erm, one of the volunteers at the youth club is sick and we won't be able to open if we don't have enough responsible adults."

"Aye, probably. I mean, yeah. I can come."

"Great, we get there at six to set up. We can talk about the library campaign?"

Her face was a beacon. "Okay, I'll fetch my new notebook and pen. I pinched it from Steve, our tutor."

Pete felt obliged to blow his empty nose. "Spot on, I'll see you then," he said, pushing the dry tissue up into his shirt sleeve.

***

After the menopause meeting Janet weaved her way back to the kitchen for a reviving cuppa.

"It's like a sauna in here," she gasped, wading through the steam.

"Janet, come here!" Tristan snapped through the clouds.

Lupin was eating a toasted teacake. "I've got something to tell you all but Tristan can go first."

Feeling like an intruder, Pete had kept himself busy by boiling both kettles and rattling cutlery. It was times like this that he thanked his lucky stars the library had self-checkout machines, considering the amount of time the staff team spent in the kitchen.

"Pete, love, are you going to do something with this steam or are you going to join us?" Janet asked, sitting down beside a fidgeting Tristan. "I've a feeling Tristan has something important to talk to us about. It's just a hunch, mind."

"Does anyone want tea?" Pete asked.

"No we don't, get your backside over here." Tristan slammed his hand on top of a buff coloured folder.

"What have you got for us, Tristan?" Lupin asked, lips smeared with butter. "You talk while I eat. Then it's my turn."

Tristan frowned and looked towards the door. "Pete, stick a chair under the door handle so nosey beggars can't get in."

Pete got up. "But there aren't any more chairs. Shall I stand?"

"Sit back down, lad," Janet ordered. "Tristan, get on with it, I've got rotas to sort."

Tristan removed some photocopied sheets from his folder. "Right, according to these meeting minutes from, eh, ages ago, there is treasure buried here."

Silence filled the steamy room.

"Where?" Lupin asked, after a moment. "On the beach?"

Janet tutted. "Why would it be on the beach?"

"Well, that's where people find it in cartoons."

"Maybe your mam and dad'll know where it is, Lupin," Pete joked.

"Not funny, Pete," Lupin sulked. "You've gotten awfully cocky for an apprentice!"

Pete recoiled. "Sorry."

Tristan threw up his hands. "It's here, or somewhere close by."

"So, like, do we have a treasure hunt?" Pete asked, desperate to lighten the mood. "Maybe it's in the lost and found box."

"There can't be treasure 'here' here," Tristan groaned. "The library was built after the minutes were recorded."

"It could be under the foundations, Tristan," Lupin sighed, licking her buttery fingers. "So, what is this treasure? Are we talking gold coins and tiaras?"

Tristan scrutinised a sheet of paper. "Let me check again."

They sat fidgeting while Tristan scanned the minutes.

After an interminable minute, he looked up. "I'm not sure what it is. Or where."

"Give it here," Janet asked, carefully pulling the papers from Tristan's reluctant hand.

"It says, "The good and honourable people of Seatown Town and Parish Council hereby claim the spoils of piracy and crime for the benefit of our necessitous community. The heinous vessel, 'The King's Maiden,' and its ill gotten gains shall dwell by Cutter's Lane. On these grounds we shall establish a seat of learning, open to all for their education and for the furtherment of decency. The elements of evil and keepers of men shall be banished, never to return."

"They're talking about my family, if you can believe it," Lupin said.

Janet reached over to pat Lupin's hand. "Aw, love. It's not *just* your family."

"Um, thanks?"

Tristan was pensive. "Are they talking about an actual ship, here, in Cutter's Lane?"

"Full of treasure," Pete whispered, eyes shining.

Lupin sat back and crossed her arms. "Well, we might find it quicker than you'd think, if you're prepared to dig up a building site."

"How so?" Janet asked her. "Oh love, is this your news?"

Lupin nodded. "According to Amanda Love, Norman Roach is buying up half of Seatown and wants to reduce the Mad Pit to rubble."

Pete was confused. "He's an elected representative. Is that not a conflict of interest?"

Before Tristan could deliver a scornful repost the kitchen door shook with four hefty raps.

"Are we living in a sitcom?" he asked the room. "Who the hell is it, now?

Keen to redeem himself, Pete boldly got up to address what lay beyond the door. "I'll get it."

Stan Tweddle stood to attention on the other side. "Brace yourselves, public servants. I've got news."

166

Janet stood up. "Stan, love, now is not the time for your complaints. Maeve's doing her best to clean up after Ernie."

"Huh, no surprise that Ernie's at the bottom of it all."

"No pun intended, eh?" Janet laughed. "Well then, what's your news that can't wait?"

"I was talking to Gavin at the Chronicle. Trying to do Ernie a good turn, as it happens."

Tristan shook his head. "Stan, what has your and Ernie's complicated bromance got to do with anything?"

"I wanted to make sure they wouldn't print my letter," he whispered, looking at Janet. "You know the one, Janet."

"I do, Stan," she replied, ignoring the bemused expressions on her colleagues' faces.

"Anyway, he said he couldn't print it in case Ernie tried to sue the paper. We had a little chat and then I went to hang up, but before I did I heard him talk to that slattern, Pam."

A confused Pete kept his mouth shut; he appreciated that Stan was building tension and reminded himself to look up the meaning of *slattern* later.

"Stan Tweddle," Janet scolded, "you can't talk about Pam…."

"Listen to me, woman," he interrupted. "She said that the library grounds are worth a fortune and that's why we're closing!"

"She said that?" Lupin crossed her arms. "What did I tell you all, eh?"

"Yes, lass," he said, practically marching on the spot with excitement. "But that it wasn't to be printed otherwise she'd lose her job."

Before anyone could comment Janet led Stan to the door and back onto the library floor. "Thank you, Stan," she whispered into his ear. "You're my number one spy now, remember."

Stan nearly choked. His brain was utterly confused and his hands shook. "Well, uh, of course, uh, anything I can do to save the Pit."

"You're doing your bit for us and it won't go unnoticed," Janet said, whipping out a tube of *Damson* gloss and painting her lips in two efficient swipes.

A sweating Stan turned on his heel and fled.

The room erupted in chatter before she could even close the kitchen door.

"Are you telling me that Stormin' Norman is planning to knock this place down to make a packet?"

168

Tristan exploded, banging his fists on the tea splattered table. "Eat the rich, I say. Who's with me?"

"I am!" shouted Pete, standing up and shooting his arm into the air, clipping the bare light bulb with his knuckles. He felt like he was in *Les Miserables.* All he needed was a drum and a guillotine.

"Where's my amethyst when I need it?" Lupin sighed, as she listened to Tristan and Pete plan their two-man revolution.

Janet sat back down. "We need to find this treasure."

Tristan stopped high-fiving Pete. "What'd you say?"

"I said, we need to find this treasure before Mr. Free Market Economy sells us to a rancid fast food franchise."

Pete was torn.

Chapter Twenty One

Malcolm was sick of getting his backside pinched.

It had been faintly amusing the first few times but now he felt like he had to have eyes in the back of his head.

He covered his buttocks every time he walked into his job at the Sheltering Oaks care home. George Garrett was the worst of them; he didn't know his own strength, despite protesting that he was a feeble octogenarian with twigs for arms.

Today it was Elsie's turn for a feel.

"Elsie, do you want me to ban you from armchair aerobics, again? I've only just got here," Malcolm complained, backing up against the foyer wall.

"I'll behave, pet, but only because I want to see you bend over," she tittered, as she inched towards the TV room on a zimmer frame bedecked in tinsel. "See you, Romeo!"

Waving her away, Malcolm knocked on the office door. He could hear giggling.

"Come on in, Mal."

He pushed open the door to find Louise bent over, her face creased with laughter. The home general manager was a five foot tall scarily efficient Scot with a warped sense of humour.

"Did you hear all that?"

"Oh, aye, made my day," she said, shaking her head. "You've left a trail of broken hearts all over this place, boyo. You're a right granny and grandad magnet."

Malcolm suddenly remembered what Ernie had said at Violet's meeting and his face coloured. "Louise, can I ask you a favour?"

"Of course, pal," she nodded, stretching to grab a box of disposable gloves from a high shelf. "I swear Stuart leaves these up here on purpose."

Malcolm reached over her head and passed her the box. "The library might close, did you know?"

"Och, that's crap," she sympathised. "When you're not working here, you're there doing whatever you do. Reading books? Flirting with pensioners?"

"Yes, amongst other things. Anyway, we've set up a campaign group to raise awareness. Maybe even keep it open."

"Why am I not surprised, Mal; you've always been the helping type."

Malcolm suddenly felt awkward. Tugging at his wavy brown hair he briefly pondered his life. Thirty-six years old and still trying to find himself. Was keeping pensioners occupied and avoiding a bruised bum what he was supposed to be doing? Why did he visit the library so much and how had he put up with Vi for so long? Was his degree in physics all for naught?

"Are you alright?" Louise asked.

He could feel her green eyes roam over his raw, exposed soul. *I need to start reading something grittier, like Game of Thrones.*

"Uh, yes," he croaked, "just got a tickle in my throat. And a mild case of existential terror. And a sore bum."

"Don't we all, Mal," Louise joked, sitting down in her oversized office chair and staring at him. "You need a change of scenery. Maybe me and you should go for a ...."

"Could we hold a tea dance in the ballroom? Like an awareness raiser?" he butted in. "According to Vi, this is mine and Tina's job. Tina couldn't come today, she's catering a funeral at St. Michael's."

Louise nodded. "Are you and Tina seeing each other?"

"No, Tina's recently widowed, poor soul. And she's a bit, you know, old for me."

Louise thumbed through her desk diary. "Poor Tina. So, when do you want to have this epic pensioner rave? There's nothing much happening on Thursdays in the big room."

"Not after the karaoke incident," Malcolm said, looking at the floor.

"Aye, not after the karaoke incident. How about a fortnight from now? That'll give you time to make your invites at craft club, eh?"

"Very funny. Yes, that would be great. Thanks Louise."

"There'd better not be any drugs at this dance," she said, marking the date onto a blank page. "And I expect a wee waltz with you."

Malcolm's face coloured. "You can put my name on your dance card."

I need to stop reading Jane Austen.

Chapter Twenty Two

The following night was juniors night at St. John's youth club. That meant thirty screaming primary school aged children sliding up and down the floor on their knees.

Courtney sat on a low brick wall outside of the church building, grasping her notebook and pen. Her brother Nathan was already inside; she could hear him wailing in the echoey hall, waiting for his fellow rioters to turn up.

"Hi, Courtney." Pete dragged his feet along the pavement, wishing with every inch of his being that he was at home watching, 'Location, Location, Location.'

"You've a face like a slapped arse. You know you can record Kirsty and Phil?"

He kicked the wall with the toe of his trainer. "Very funny. Is someone already in the hall?"

"Aye, Nathan's warming up."

"You know we can't allow kids in there without adult supervision, Court," he moaned.

Courtney stood up. "The Rev's inside mopping up this morning's rain, he's keeping an eye on him."

Tutting, Pete led Courtney into the main space, nervously outlining her responsibilities as they went. She scribbled into her notebook, disappointed that she was expected to work.

"... so, don't let anyone into the kitchen because we can't afford to lose any more teabags."

She stopped. "Kids are nicking teabags?"

"They stuff them down the sink holes and turn on the taps."

Both turned to watch Nathan skid through the Reverend's freshly mopped floor, his squeaking trainers rattling every ear drum in the vicinity. Pete winced, "Holy…"

"What was that, Pete?" the Reverend asked, pushing his mop and bucket towards the store. "I can't hear you over the racket, ha ha."

"SHUT UP AND SIT DOWN, NATHAN!" Courtney shrieked, grabbing the neck of her brother's football shirt and hauling him over to a nearby gym mat. Conscious of the watching Reverend she reached out and ruffled Nathan's hair. "Good lad."

The Reverend wiped his hands on his bleach wash jeans. "Hello, Courtney, are you helping out tonight? That's great, we could really do with the help. The noise, you know? It gets to you. But very important work, yes?"

"Em, yeah?" Courtney replied, mentally backing her way out of the hall and into the cosy confines of her bedroom. In her head she was buried under her duvet scoffing a Mars Bar and watching, 'Don't Tell The Bride."

What followed was eighty minutes of intense regret; way worse than the time she'd applied sixty layers of mascara for a dare. She'd been handed a plastic spoon and asked to remove tea leaf gunk from the toilet sinks.

Courtney tapped Pete on the shoulder. "Pete, I want to go home right now and never come back here, but can we talk about our library campaign first?"

An ashen Pete turned around to face her. "A ten year-old just gave me a wedgie, Court. Um, shall we go outside?"

"Hell, yes. Take me far, far away," she cackled, watching the Reverend shove empty energy drinks bottles into a plastic bin bag. "Sorry, Rev!"

"Thanks for your help, Courtney," he yelled. "Maybe we'll see you next week?"

Before she could impolitely decline, Pete grasped her wrist and pulled her out of the door.

"You don't want to get sucked into this, Court," Pete complained. "Seriously, you'll never be able to leave."

They stood against the back wall of the church and gathered their breath.

"Now that I'm outside, I think I kind of enjoyed myself," Courtney mused, wiping tea-stained hands onto her leggings. "It's weird because when I was inside, I hated it."

"That's how it gets you," he warned.

She turned towards him. "So, uh, are we going to get on with this? It's just I didn't picture doing it behind the church hall."

"Doing what?" Pete asked, edging back a millimeter. His face was a contorted blend of confusion and elation.

"Planning our extreme eating contest, you idiot."

He exhaled. "I think it should be sausage rolls."

"So you can enter?"

"Well, maybe. Am I allowed to?"

"Dunno. We should do it in the library and when we've got people there, we can lock the doors and refuse to let them out until the council agrees to our terms."

Pete cocked an eyebrow. "Have you been talking to Ernie?"

"Ugh, no. I dreamt about it, actually."

"Um, how about we ask them to sign a petition instead. That way we'll avoid getting arrested. I don't think Helen could cope with a night in the slammer."

Courtney nodded. "Yeah, she wouldn't approve of those orange jumpsuits. Not her colour, at all."

They both looked at each other and laughed.

Pete pointed at her jacket pocket. "Where's your notebook and pen? Shouldn't we be taking minutes?"

"What? Oh, yeah," she mumbled, pulling the worn notebook from her coat. *We had a moment. Did we have a moment?*

Flipping onto a fresh page, Courtney scribbled down the date and time and marked them both as present.

"You've got nice handwriting for a girl," Pete said. *What does that even mean?*

"Better than yours," she snorted. "You write like you're wearing a pair of boxing gloves."

"For your information, I write like my grandad."

"Was he a boxer?"

Pete stuffed his hands in his pockets and stalked towards the footpath, forcing Courtney to follow him. "Aw, sorry Pete. You make me nervous!"

He swiveled round. "I make *you* nervous? You've got to be joking."

"What? I make *you* nervous? How?"

Pete eyeballed her, unsure if she was joking. "Because you're dead confident. Obviously."

"Obviously," Courtney joked, looking down at the gum-splattered pavement. "You know, there's nothing wrong with being confident, Pete." She looked up at him and grinned. "You should try it sometime."

"So, em, how do I make you nervous?" Pete asked.

Courtney bent down to tie her shoelace. "You're an apprentice. You've got your life sorted. And, I fancy you a little bit."

"Oh."

"'Oh'. Come on, Pete. Is that it?"

They stood and watched as an ice cream van hurtled past, a dozen kids trailing behind it, waving their hands and shouting.

Pete nudged her trainer with his boot. "Do you fancy a cornetto?"

Chapter Twenty Three

At four a.m. the following morning Stan Tweddell sat up in bed and rubbed his sleep-encrusted eyes.

"Did I hear them say there was *pirate treasure* in the library?"

Flopping back down onto his pillow he swiftly returned to sleep, to dream of mermaids that looked like Bev Rogers.

As Stan battled with sirens, Maeve was pushing a mop across the sticky floor of the 'Drunken Sailor.'

"Quizzers are filthy animals," she muttered into the thick, dimly lit silence.

Scrubbing the pub wasn't without its merits; it paid for her daughter's university accommodation and it allowed her to watch over 'The King's Maiden', the dusty ship that peered at her from its high, neglected shelf.

Tonight, things would change.

The ship was going home with her; one port closer to its final dock.

Chapter Twenty Four

Despite a very public refusal to adopt modern technology, Norman Roach had two mobile phones.

One was for business, and one was for 'business'.

The 'business' phone buzzed in his pocket during point seven of the waste prevention oversight and scrutiny committee meeting agenda.

With slick sleight of hand, he slid the phone under the board room table and onto his lap. Ian had reset the device's settings to vibrate and reduced the screen's brightness, so Norman could conduct under-table business with ease. The only fly in the ointment was his failing eyesight and a tendency to send shopping lists, not to his wife, but to nefarious building contractors.

A brisk voice echoed around the small meeting room. "Now then, let's move on to the misuse of our new plastic and glass recycling boxes. My neighbour's using his box to grow potatoes, which is commendable but not the intended use for this scheme."

As his fingers worked, Norman smiled and nodded towards the meeting chair and Director of Community Services, Pauline Graves.

"Norman, any thoughts?" Pauline asked, zeroing in on the councillor. "Don't tell us you've been growing veg in yours too?"

A rumble of laughter erupted from the group of seven members.

For crying out loud. "Vegetables? What are those?" he joked. "As you're all aware my concern has been with the prohibitive cost of this recycling box roll-out."

Pauline checked the agenda on her tablet. "You'll get your chance shortly, Norman; that's point eight. Right, folks, should we consider an educational social media campaign?"

Norman grunted and returned to his phone.

"*We need to move quickly on the Mad Pit. There's not much time…*"

The phone slipped from his sweaty hand and landed on the carpeted floor with a muffled *clonk*.

"Wha'? Who's increasing council tax?"

Pauline rapped the table with her biro. "Can you repeat that, Norman? We couldn't quite hear you under there."

Norman tapped out another message. *"C you at bowls ltr."*

Emerging from the balmy pond of trousered legs, Norman casually straightened his hair and resumed his position as a fine, upstanding member of the community.

"My shoelace has been undone since lunch; it was driving me crackers," he said, staring directly at Pauline. "I'm awfully thirsty, Pauline. Are you going to make us all a cuppa?

Chapter Twenty Five

A gusty wind whipped around the Lighthouse Theatre, a fading detached two-storey building said to be haunted by the ghost of Sadie, a bitter seamstress who was jilted at the altar by Max, a mediocre understudy.

Maeve tutted at the empty crisp bags circling her feet by the front door. Crouching down, she peered inside for evidence of broken glass, and, satisfied that they contained nothing but crumbs and saliva, despatched them into her pocket for binning later.

She rang a doorbell smeared with fingerprints, and waited.

"Hello?"

"Alright, Aiden? It's Maeve; have you got 5?"

"Hi love, come on in."

The door buzzed and Maeve pushed her way into a shabby foyer plastered in peeling posters promoting plays, pantomimes and glistening male dance troupes.

On weekends the miniscule box office housed Winnie O'Neill, the ferocious ticket manager who had once famously barred a comedian from their own show because he had pinched a teenage usherette on the bottom.

As she zipped up the rickety stairs towards Aiden's office she was pleased to find the bannisters free of dust and detritus.

She pushed open the door marked, 'Theatre Manager' and found Aiden Lawson bent over a stage plan.

"I just don't know where to place the chorus. Baritones generally stand in the back row but Ted is only five feet two." He straightened his back and turned to face Maeve. "Sheryl the soprano will dwarf him."

"Why've you got a chorus in 'The Secret Diary of Adrian Mole?"

He scratched his head. "To give our director a migraine?"

"You're a demon, Aiden," she laughed, plopping onto a worn chair that offered uninterrupted views of the Irish sea. *It won't be long until this is replaced with apartments.*

"I know," he said, clapping his hands. "I'll get Derek to build a nice platform for Ted and the tenors."

"Aye, that'll keep Del off your back, for sure," Maeve nodded, removing a tissue from her coat pocket and wiping a set of wind chimes that clanked against the grimy window pane. "These are out of tune, Aiden. You know, I'm absolutely gasping."

"Oh, yes. I'll just put the kettle on." He left Maeve to her cleaning and hurried into the small kitchen that ran parallel to the office.

"I get the feeling you're here about something momentous, Maeve!" he yelled from the steamy room, his voice diminished by the rumbling of an industrial boiler.

"What makes you say that?" Maeve asked, padding into the humidity. She reached into the fridge, pulled out a carton of oat milk and emptied a healthy dollop into two clean mugs Aiden had retrieved from the ageing dishwasher.

"You know, that boiler works harder than any of us," Aiden laughed. "Builder's tea, right?"

"Is there any other kind?" she asked. "I put the milk in first, don't kill me."

Laughing, Aiden took the mugs and filled them with spitting hot water.

"Lupin's very worried, you know," he said, proffering a mug to Maeve.

Maeve reached out and accepted the mug of beige tea. It wasn't quite as strong as she'd have liked but she appreciated Aiden's gesture, a man more familiar with thyme than Tetley's.

"So I've heard."

"From your little network of Mad Pit guardians, I suppose?"

Maeve raised her eyebrows.

"Sorry, Maeve, I didn't mean that," he said, taking a sip. "From what she's told me, there's information out there that'll show us in an unwelcome light."

"I know it don't mean much but try not to worry," she reassured him. "You and your family are good people, everyone around here knows that."

Aiden stared out of the kitchen window. "The Lawsons were slave traders and pirates, Maeve. We'll hardly be appearing on, 'Who Do You Think You Are?' any time soon."

"I might have something that'll cheer you up, Aiden."

Aiden tapped his forehead with a damp teaspoon. "I'm veggie, Maeve, so there's no point trying to convince me to eat one of Eileen's sausage rolls again."

Maeve started to rifle inside her bag, then thought better of it. "Don't tell anyone but Elieen's experimenting with vegan sausage rolls. It'll cause *such* a scandal."

"She is?" Aiden's face was a picture of childlike joy. "That *has* cheered me up, Maeve, thank you."

"That's not what I was going to tell you, Aiden," she said, backing out of the kitchen. "I know I'm being dead cryptic, but tell your Lupin that the Lawsons will come out of this a-okay."

Aiden screwed up his eyes."Your aura is sparkling, Maeve. Are you part-fairy? I won't tell anyone, if you are."

"I've got a bag full of fairy dust here, Aiden," she said, slapping the side of her bag. "Maybe it'll save us all, eh?"

As she left the theatre Maeve spotted Ernie in his usual spot, a bashed up wooden bench next to the boat repair shed.

Youngsters huddled by the harbourside, blasting terrible music on tinny speakers and punching each other on the shoulder.

Couples meandered around the harbour perimeter, getting in their steps and holding serious conversations about relationships, recipes and furniture shopping.

Maeve inhaled the mingling scents of oil and seawater.

While Ernie's head was turned she side-stepped to the back of the bench and tapped him on the shoulder. "Good evening, sir. Can I talk to you about your recent car accident? You may be eligible for compensation."

Ernie shuddered, forcing Celeste to scurry from her warm spot on his shoulder into the hood of his ancient anorak. "Flipping heck, Maeve," he scolded. "You had me doubting myself! Do I drive? Do I not?"

"Shove up, lad," she ordered, making a sweeping motion with her hands. "Give a lady a seat."

"Seeing as there's no lady here, I might as well give you one," he said, sliding his skinny buttocks along the damp wooden seat. "You're not getting any younger, after all."

"You don't mellow with age, do you?" she laughed, sniffing the space between them. "What on earth have you been eating?"

Ernie reached back to gently retrieve Celeste, the mellow coastal wind ruffling the rat's short, brown fur. "She's been scoffing a freshly hatched chicken nugget, kindly donated by Zach of the Market Place Posse."

Maeve carefully patted the rat's tiny skull. "Aw, if only the newspapers would cover heart-warming local stories like this, instead of bin disputes and strikes."

"Ha ha, very funny," he scoffed, placing Celeste in his anorak pocket. "Why are you here, anyway? You're putting off the ladies."

"What? Do you come here to pick up women?" Maeve asked, fascinated.

"Sometimes. Depends."

"On what?"

"Well, if the women's speed walking club picks the harbour for a route."

"But aren't they moving too fast for you to flirt with them?"

"Nay lass, this is where they finish," he said, tapping his forehead with a grimy index finger.

Maeve opened her bag, gently removed the kitten-sized ship and cradled it on her lap. Gleaming from a thorough scrub the vessel was ready to take to the waves once more.

"That lass wants to get back on the water," Ernie commented, pointing at the curvaceous painted figurehead. "And she needs covering up. Can't you paint a cossy on her?"

"That could be a job for Vi's craft club," Maeve laughed, giving the main mast a rub with the sleeve of her sweater. "I think she's beautiful. Aren't you, my lovely?"

The pair watched as a gaggle of speed walkers advanced towards them, a blur of swinging arms, silver bobs and gaudy fleece jackets.

"Lot of big empty houses up there, eh?" Ernie said, pointing towards the smattering of white townhouses that loomed over Seatown. Once grand residences of old industrial giants, only empty shells remained, attracting pigeons and cider-drinking kids.

Maeve sighed. "Rich men built this town, ruined this town and deserted this town, Ernie."

"That's a bit harsh, missus," Ernie started, before turning to offer his fan club a royal wave. "Afternoon, ladies! Is that a new top, Brenda?"

"Oh, Ernie," Maeve laughed, shaking her head.

The giggling troupe sauntered away, chugging water as they went.

"I could have pulled there; now they'll think we're courting."

Ignoring him, Maeve pulled out a folded cotton shopper from her handbag and carefully placed 'The King's Maiden' inside it.

"Stop looking at Brenda's backside and look at me, young man," Maeve asked Ernie.

Ernie did as he was told.

"I need you to take 'The King's Maiden' and give it to Tristan. Can you do that?"

"I know you left that tatty old box in the bin for me," Ernie sniffed, accepting the bag. "Why don't you just give all of this to them yourself?"

Maeve slumped against the bench. "None of this can come from me. My name isn't respected in these parts."

"Whaddya mean? You're not related to our Lupin, are you?

"No, I'm not." She took Ernie's hand. "You know, the Lawsons weren't the only ones responsible for what happened here. And that lovely family has paid its dues over and over again."

Ernie was conflicted. An attractive woman was holding his hand yet he felt it more appropriate to ignore this obvious come-on and focus on the momentous task; he felt dizzy.

"Are you alright, lad? You look a bit peaky?"

"I'm right as rain," he reassured her, anxious to get straight to the gossip. "So who are you? I've not heard owt bad about the Watsons, other than Big Jim who's in Haverigg for stealing tellys."

Maeve cracked a crooked smile. "I didn't start life as a Watson. I've been married twice, then I left the area for fifteen years and returned to Seatown and met John, five years ago."

"You know, you could have just changed your name by deed poll. So, John's a Watson?

"Aye, he's Big Jim's little brother."

Ernie hid his blushes by checking on Celeste.

Maeve stood up. "Look, it doesn't matter who I am, or was. The goal is to get this ship to Tristan. Tell him you found it...here, at the harbour."

Ernie scanned the gum-splattered path before pointing to a bin. "What about there?"

"Perfect," Maeve said, reaching out to shake his hand. "Keep her safe, Ernie. And don't be selling her to buy cigarettes."

Ernie took her hand and kissed it. "I've given up, didn't you know?"

"Oh?"

"Aye, I smoke cigars now. I'm dead posh, me."

Chapter Twenty Six

"I'm going to be late for my course," Courtney complained.

"I'm going to be late for my actual job," Pete snapped. "That's worse."

Both trailed the back of a chatty queue that had meandered out of 'The La'al Teacake' and onto the pavement.

Pete looked up at a rapidly darkening sky, silently urging Eileen to get a move on before his heavily gelled hair and thin cotton shirt got a soaking. "Why does she have to talk to every single customer?"

"Because she's nice," Courtney snapped. "And dead nosey."

Smiling pensioners shuffled out of the bakery bearing bags of fruit scones and a week's worth of gossip.

"Finally," Pete muttered, stepping over the threshold as the first drops of rain struck his back. He glanced at the soon-to-be-saturated elderly shoppers, feeling an urge to help, but today the business of sausage rolls would have to overrule good deeds.

Eileen flicked a damp rag over the counter, bouncing crumbs off Pete's navy tie. "Hello, love birds," she cooed. "Aren't you an attractive pair?"

"One of us is," Courtney joked.

Pete felt the need to assert himself. "I'm here about sausage, Eileen," he said, slapping the counter with his hand.

"Aren't we all, lovely," Eileen smirked, throwing a wink at Courtney. "I've got an offer on big white baps, if you're interested, sonny?"

Courtney tried to steer the conversation from filth to fun. "Eileen, are you on HRT?"

"I am, lass," she laughed, reaching over the counter for a high five. "I feel amazing. And you know who else is on it? Only…"

Pete stepped in front of Courtney's raised hand. "Sorry, Eileen. We've only got a minute before I start work and Courtney starts her, uh, …"

"...mental health first aid."

"Yeah, that. Anyway, we want to organise a 'How Many Sausage Rolls Can You Eat in 10 Minutes' awareness-raiser."

Eileen looked confused. "To raise awareness of what? High cholesterol?"

Courtney smacked her forehead with the palm of her hand. "No, the library! It might be closing, Eileen."

"So you need sausage rolls? I take it Greggs turned you down?"

Pete studied a congregation of raisins on the floor. "Yeah, company policy."

"Yours are far nicer, Eileen," Courtney beamed. "Can you help us? It'll be a great advert for the shop, eh?"

A sweating middle-aged man bombed into the bakery waving a crumpled shopping list. "Sorry, I'm in a disc zone. Can I have a dozen wholemeal rolls and a sliced granary loaf, please?"

Eileen waved Courtney and Pete out of the shop. "I'll give you your sausage rolls. Now, if you're not going to spend any money, get out of my shop."

At five minutes past ten, Janet ushered a bemused Pete and Lupin into the staff kitchen.

"Gerrin, you two," Janet whispered, scanning the library floor for Violet-shaped trouble.

Tristan sat at the table chewing a sparkly purple biro.

"Tristan, that's my pen you're dribbling on," Lupin cried. "Throw it in the sink and wash it, please."

"Hush up, Topsy and Tim." Shutting the door, Janet deftly grabbed a chair and placed its head under the handle.

"I think that only works in the movies, Janet," Pete said. "I can't see it stopping Violet."

"Movies," Tristan mumbled, running Lupin's biro under the hot water tap. "They were called films in my day."

"You're only forty-one, Tristan," Lupin remarked, lightly punching him on the arm. "Ooh, sorry. I forgot you had arthritis."

Tristan rubbed his arm. "Janet, we need to get a move on. Seatown WI is coming shortly to record local ghost stories."

"The life you lead, Tristan. Right, sit down, all of you, we can't leave the floor empty for long."

Four necks swivelled as the doorknob rattled.

"Must be one of your ghosts, Tristan," Janet said. "Tell them to wait until I'm done."

"It's just the wind, Pete left the main door on the latch."

Pete gasped. "I did not!"

"It's like herding cats," Janet moaned. "Right, who wants to spend the night looking for hidden treasure?"

Everyone nodded.

Tristan waved his hand in the air. "Miss, miss! Since we're searching for ill-gotten gains, I vote that we buy up 'Best Booze's' stock of rum and have a party."

"I don't think that's very appropriate, Tristan," Lupin said. "I vote we buy beer."

Pete timidly raised a hand. "And cheese and onion crisps?"

"Granted," declared Janet. "Oh, and don't tell anyone on the community services team that we're staying late. But if anyone asks, we're doing a stock take."

***

Holding the bag away from his body with pinched fingers, the man crept into the library.

For once, he was grateful that the building was quiet; interfering biddies were not conducive to a successful mission.

But it was too quiet.

Where's Trichia when you need him?

Looking left to right, he gingerly approached the kitchen and rattled the doorknob. Nothing doing. Complete silence.

Bugger. Mission:impossible.

Desperate to divest himself of the package, Ernie elected the path of least resistance. *To the bog I go.*

Chapter Twenty Seven

As the morning progressed, the threat of mild debauchery permeated every book, leaflet and ancient desktop computer in the library.

Violet was the first to comment on the unfamiliar frisson, a condition more likely to be found at mid-week bingo in the United Reformed Church, not in one of the town's oldest and most venerated public buildings.

"Do you think they're up to something?"

The creative writing club was engrossed in a ten-minute free writing exercise. Tina scribbled as if in a trance, her pen digging into the paper like a tiny dagger. Helen wrote in dainty cursive with her eyes closed, humming an off-key tune. The whole scene was reminiscent of a Victorian seance, minus the table knocking.

"Is anybody listening to me?" She stood and surveyed her domain, eyes peeled for misdemeanours. "Can you not feel it?"

Helen threw down her pencil. "I was getting somewhere there, Vi! What on earth are you talking about?"

Violet took a seat and planted her elbows on the paper-strewn table. "There's meddling in this library. And where *is* everyone today?"

Tina rubbed out her most recent sentence. "Now I've made a mistake, Vi. We still have two minutes of writing left!"

"Why are you so narky, Tina?" Helen grumbled. "Mal's working, Vi."

Violet sighed. "I know he's not an official club member but I miss Ernie."

"I saw him fly down High Street earlier waving an empty bag around," Helen said. "Probably on his way to the tip for some new clothes."

"Sorry, you two," Tina said, rubbing her eyes. "There was a massive fight at the birthday I catered last night. I had to follow the booker around for hours until he would pay me."

"Was it an eighteenth?"

Tina yawned. "No, it was my neighbour's ninetieth. Those old folk had some serious grievances going back *decades.* I'm knackered, I've never served so much pavlova."

"Easy on the gums, isn't it?" Helen said, running her manicured hand down the length of a delicate silk scarf in a fetching shade of blue.

"There's electricity in the air, ladies," Violet hissed. "And it's not that annoying dehumidifier."

Helen shook her head. "That was Mal's fault…"

"...you were the one that knocked over the water fountain, Helen. You shouldn't visit the library after a boozy lunch."

Violet struck the table top with a stray pencil. "We need to snoop."

Tina snatched it from Violet's hand. "You've probably broken the lead. Thanks a bunch, Vi."

***

A rumpled train of over-stimulated four-year-olds snaked its way through the doorway, herded by two nursery school workers wearing tired smiles.

Violet pushed her way between sticky fingers and pigtails to reach Lupin, who was brandishing four different percussion instruments.

"Lupin, love, have you got a minute?" she asked, side-stepping a selection of patched-up bean bags.

Lupin puffed out her cheeks. "Vi, does it look like I have a minute? My volunteer has rang in sick so unless you're prepared to be Mrs. Tambourine Woman, I can't help you."

Violet gurned. "I've got no rhythm."

A tiny person with spiky black hair approached. "Miss, the yellow bean bag looks like my baby brother's poo. Can I sit beside Asif, today?"

Lupin pointed at a purple beanbag. "Will that one do you, Andrew? Pull it up alongside Asif."

"Yeah! That one looks like *my* poo!" The boy ran hand in hand with his friend and they both threw themselves onto their bean bags in a fit of giggles.

"Now they'll all want to swop bean bags and the staff will pretend not to notice, because it's ten-thirty in the morning and they're already exhausted."

Lupin handed Violet a tambourine. "Just keep in time and you'll be fine. Ha, that was a rhyme!" She did a mini star jump. "And so was that!"

"Um, Lupin, I'm not sure I can help you," Violet moaned, searching the floor for a good samaritan. "I'm not used to bairns. Actually, I just wanted to ask you about something. You're all awfully jumpy today. Why is that?"

"Vi," Lupin countered. "You've not had a police check for kids' activities but you can still help me as long as you don't leave my side. That means your only responsibility is keeping rhythm for half a dozen nursery rhymes."

"Well, in that case...I'm sure Tina and Helen can manage without me for a bit."

Lupin patted Violet's springy indigo perm. "Thank you Vi, you will be richly rewarded in your next life."

"Hmmm."

$$***$$

Thirty minutes later Violet stumbled back to her seat with one less cardigan button, mumbling 'The Wheels on the Bus' and thanking her lucky stars that her only dependant was a small dog.

Chapter Twenty Eight

That night...

Pete stood in front of the mirror, modelling the black balaclava he had inherited from his father, one of dozens churned out by his nana during the great Cumbrian chill of 1985.

Ignoring the faint scent of male scalp, he concentrated on looking badass, striking James Bond poses that were barely visible in the smudged glass.

It never once occurred to him that he had every legitimate reason to be in his own workplace after hours. He just really wanted to wear the balaclava. And maybe use a torch.

Lupin piled polished crystals into her skirt pockets; her pretty armoury against unfettered capitalism.

After splitting a can of smoked mackerel with her cat, she pulled on her duffle coat, grabbed the garden trowel from the cupboard under the sink, and set off for the library.

Tristan delicately slid the library floor plans into a fresh poly pocket and popped them into his satchel.

The dark, cavernous interior of his second favourite man bag housed a maglite torch, a banana sandwich, two bars of Galaxy, a notebook purloined from the Seatown Council reception stationery cupboard, three biros, four plastic evidence bags (sandwich bags, in another life), a bottle of Gaviscon and a vintage stanley knife.

He fingered the rim of his fedora. Purchased on a whim in Malaga, its day had come. "Yeah, Indiana's ready."

***

Janet's belly was gurgling.

She'd just demolished a fairly tasty but very runny ham and mushroom omelette, lovingly prepared by Adam. He'd hovered over her as she ate, bursting with barely concealed pride at his culinary prowess.

I'll be fine, Tristan will have some Gaviscon in his handbag.

Dropping a kiss on Adam's cheek, she tried not to get too excited about finding loot in her library.

"See you later, love."

Adam shouted at her disappearing back. "Don't come home draped in pearls, love. Put them in your handbag, else you'll be mugged."

Chapter Twenty Nine

The giggling treasure seekers needlessly slipped into the library through the back door.

Barring the band of Men in Sheds members stalking Cutter's Lane with planks of two-by-four, the mean streets of Seatown were quiet. "They're making birdhouses for St. Mary's primary school," Lupin reported.

"Your Adam should join up, Janet," Tristan joked. "He's good with his hands, isn't he?"

Pete didn't know where to look and stumbled into an 'Animals in Literature' display stand.

Janet punched Tristan on the bicep. "He's only fifty, you little sod. God, your arms are puny."

"Knock on your torches and keep hush," Lupin said, peering into the dark depths of Hobbies and Crafts, half expecting an elected member to pounce from the shadows.

Pete shook off his rucksack and removed a large torch. "This is my uncle's garden shed torch. He uses it to look for hedgehogs."

"Why?" Tristan asked, carefully retrieving his stanley knife from a battered tupperware lunchbox.

"Because hedgehogs are adorable," Lupin said, turning to stare at Pete. "Pete, love, why do you look like a terrorist?"

Pete shrugged. "I didn't want anyone to recognise me."

"And why on earth have you got a stanley knife, Tristan?" Janet laughed.

Tristan slumped onto a nearby chair and dangled the knife between his fingers. "Look, have any of us thought about where this so-called treasure might be?"

"Well, it might be buried between the walls," Janet said. "Or hidden in the cellar."

Pete was puzzled. "We have a cellar?"

Tristan jiggled his knife against a bookshelf. "But won't it have been buried underground, before the library was built?"

"Maybe, maybe not," Janet admitted. "Maybe people looked after it until the time was right to move it."

"You mean kept it at home, stashed behind their silverware?"

"Or under their kiddie's bed," Janet sighed. "What on earth are we doing? Do any of us actually believe there's treasure here? Wouldn't someone have found it by now? And why are we dressed in disguise, holding torches? We're allowed to be here!"

While Lupin Googled 'Madeleine Pit Library hidden treasure,' Tristan spread the library floor plans out onto the craft club trestle table.

"The only thing Google has thrown up is Bev Rogers."

Pete screwed up his face. "Yuck."

"Young man, according to The Seatown Chronicle, Bev Rodgers is the Mad Pit's hidden treasure owing to her decades of fundraising for library activities."

The two intrepid explorers looked at each other and laughed.

"To be fair, she's a treasure for putting up with Stan Tweddle's very obvious disgust everytime she walks past him."

Tristan placed a hefty encyclopedia on each corner of the ground floor plan. "That's because Stan clearly fancies her."

Janet looked over Tristan's shoulder. "Right, what are we looking at, Indiana?"

"I'm really not sure," Tristan admitted.

"We're buggered, aren't we?"

"Yes."

Lupin slipped her phone back into her bag. "Why don't we go to the pub quiz?"

Janet nodded. "Best idea you've had all week, Lup."

Carefully refolding the floor plans, Tristan visualised the pint of stout that would alleviate his embarrassment. *Harrison Ford's got nothing to worry about.*

"I'll meet you outside, I need to use the loo."

Lupin grimaced. "Alright, Tristan, no need to tell us your life story."

***

Tristan massaged lurid pink liquid soap into his wet hands and rinsed.

He looked at himself in the mirror. *Indiana Jones and the Raiders of the Failing Library.*

Grabbing a handful of paper towels, he dried his hands and lobbed the wet wad into the bin.

Back to the drawing board, lad.

From its vantage point on the bottom shelf of the baby changing table, Ernie's package watched as Tristan and his fedora exited the building.

Chapter Thirty

Pete was ashamed of his hangover.

Today, he had sausage rolls to wrangle, media to engage and Courtney to impress, all while nursing an insidious headache that was determined to bore a hole from his left eye into his brain.

Pete was man enough to accept that drinking was best left to the professionals. Like Tristan, whose ten pints manifested in a light sheen of sweat and bouts of impulsive hugging.

They may have won the quiz but Janet's tone deaf rendition of 'We are the champions' didn't win them any new fans.

And last orders saw Lupin hopping around the bar pretending to be a one-legged pirate called 'Lawson the Lunatic,' dragging Pete behind her as her pet parrot, 'Pretty Petey'.

———————————— *** ————————————

"Right, meeting time," Courtney said, pulling Pete into an empty meeting room.

She was wearing black trousers, a white shirt and black trainers.

Pete looked at her. "Have you got a job waitressing?"

"No, you idiot!" she cried, slapping his arm. "I'm trying to look corporate, aren't I?"

Pete paled and felt the room tilt. "Oh."

"Are you poorly? You look like you've seen a ghost." She rubbed his arm, trying to remove the slap. "Sorry I hit you. I'm nervous."

He sat down. "It's alright, Court. We went to the 'Drunken Sailor' last night and I disgraced myself."

Courtney rolled her eyes. "Didn't see you falling for beer pressure, Pete. I'm shocked."

"Yeah, me too. I watched Tristan knock back rum, slap his thighs and call himself a buccaneer." He was desperate for a pint of iced water. "Why are you nervous?"

She leaned against a patchy wall covered in faded posters. "Well, I suppose I'd like a job, yeah? Bring in some money."

"You want to make a good impression tomorrow, don't you?"

"Course I do! And don't go entering the competition. It's for serious sausage roll eaters only."

"I can't, I'm not allowed," he grumbled. "Work policy."

Courtney pulled up a to-do list on her phone. "Right, we've got to pick up the sausage rolls from Eileen. Have you emptied the staff fridge?"

"Yeah, and Janet's not impressed. She's got nowhere for her probiotic yogurts."

"Tough. Anyway, I've booked the Chronicle photographer and she says they're waiting on your press release. Have you emailed it to Gavin?"

Pete nodded. "Yeah, at half-three this morning. I woke up my brother and got him to check it for mistakes. He said it was fine and then he gave me a dead arm."

"Oh my God, Pete! You should have let a grown-up read it first!"

"He is a grown-up, calm down!" Sweat drenched Pete's back. "Janet helped me put the guest list together. Guess who's coming?"

Courtney tutted. "Cockroach?"

"Yeah, so we'll need to keep an eye on him," Pete shouted over the sound of his palpitating heart. "He's up to no good."

Crossing her arms, Courtney grinned. "This'll be a laugh, I can't wait."

"Hmmmm."

"Gimme a high five, Petey boy!" she laughed, thrusting her hand in front of Pete's pale face.

Pete sunk to his haunches and dry heaved. "I think I might call in sick."

"Wisht, I smell Bev," she whispered, cracking open the door.

A mist of hairspray wafted into the small room followed by a grinning head.

"Hiya, doll!"

Bev Rogers strode inside carrying an industrial sized bucket of ketchup. "We thought this would help the sausage rolls go down a bit better."

"Erm, no brown sauce, then?" Pete asked, watching her heft the bucket about with ease.

"Get away, you cheeky beggar," she said, rapping the plastic lid. "Courtesy of Seatown Rotary Club. I'll see you in the morning with a job lot of serviettes."

Courtney was stunned. "Thanks, Bev."

"You're welcome, doll," the woman said. "Now then, I'm off to hunt down Stan Tweddle. If you hear squealing, don't come running."

And with that, Bev and her pungent hairspray left the room.

Crouched under the reception desk, Janet clasped an ice cold can of cola in one hand and two paracetamol in the other. She quickly necked the pain relieving drugs, hopeful that they would start working immediately on her thumping headache.

On her slow ascent the phone rang.

"Flippin' heck," she gasped. "That's loud."

Janet assumed a professional stance, ignoring the impending vertigo that threatened to tip her into the filing cabinet.

"Madeleine Pit Library, hello?"

"You've made my life very difficult."

Janet could hear frantic brushing. "Amanda?"

The sound of a clattering hairbrush filled Janet's ears. "Norman Roach is up to no good. Did you know that?"

Janet sat down. "Erm, yes. We're aware that he has plans for us."

Amanda tutted. "So what are we going to do about it?"

"Are you on our side, Amanda?" Janet asked, eyes wide.

"He always stands so close to me, Janet. And his jokes are terrible." She paused. "But his daughter's worse."

"Janine? Why?"

"She needs a brand new building for her cosmetic surgery salon and she wants it on your street. I didn't tell you that."

As the line went dead and Janet replaced the receiver she pondered how her day could get any stranger.

***

Stan Tweddle carefully typed 'How to save a library" into the search engine. Before taking his seat, Stan had removed a pack of antibacterial wipes from his coat pocket and disinfected the doorknob, the keyboard, the chair, the table and the computer screen.

Walking into the computer suite Bev's nostrils snagged the sharp scent of Dettol.

"Do you know, Stan, your old undercrackers would make *great* dusters. Why don't you keep a pair in your pervy trench coat for cleaning emergencies?"

"Away, Ariel! I'm busy with serious, um, business."

Bev cocked her head. "Ariel? Why not Persil?"

Stan pushed all thoughts of mermaids from his cluttered mind. "Nevermind, I meant to say Jezebel. You're distracting me."

He returned to his typing.

Bev draped her tracksuited form on a neighbouring computer chair and twirled towards Stan.

"Stan, love?"

Stan held his breath, determined not to inhale any deadly hormones. The last time he'd been in such close proximity to a woman was during his five-yearly visit to the dentist.

Ms. Coombe was fragrant and respectful, not a deadly succubus of the Bev Rogers variety. And she'd transformed his gnashers into something passable. What had Bev ever done for him, other than make him feel uncomfortable?

"Earth to Tweddle?"

"What do you want?" he seethed, pointing to his screen. "Can't you see I'm single-handedly keeping this place open?"

Bev seized his arm with a manicured hand. "I think a stunt is in order."

"What are you on about, woman?" he asked, shaking her off.

"You and me have got form, lad. We're media savvy, you know?"

Stan had to admit that she was speaking the truth. Without Bev and Stan, The Seatown Chronicle would be full of adverts for mobility scooters.

"And?"

Bev leaned in closer. "And we're overdue a collaboration."

_____ *** _____

Restacking the Cookery section with Jamie and Nigella, Janet watched Stan Tweddle and Bev Rogers leave the computer suite.

They were deep in conversation and she swore she heard Stan laugh.

"Yep. That'll be it."

Chapter Thirty One

Saturday morning arrived and with it a refreshed Pete, who had spent the previous night diluting his blood alcohol levels with decaffeinated tea.

"Thank God you don't look dead," Courtney shouted, skipping towards Pete as he opened the library door.

"You're in a good mood," he said, knocking off the ground floor alarm and checking the library for signs of scruffiness. The place was gleaming. *Maeve's been in early.*

"This is the earliest I've got up on a Saturday since I went nicking carrots with my granddad."

Pete rolled his eyes. "I'll not ask."

"Best not. He's been banned from every allotment in West Cumbria."

The duo made their way to the kitchen, ready to prep for the sausage roll extravaganza.

Before Pete could switch on the light the aroma of pork and pastry forced them both to turn their heads.

Eileen ambled in carrying a steaming box. "Anyone for fifty of Seatown's finest sausage rolls?"

Pete rushed forward, arms outstretched. "D'you need a hand, Eileen?"

"Away lad, I didn't win the county shot put shield for nothing. Where do you want them?"

Courtney cleared space on the kitchen table. "Here would be fab, thanks Eileen."

Eileen placed the box on the table along with a few sachets of salt and pepper.

"People like seasoning, even when they're not taking the time to taste what's going in their mush."

"Thanks again, Eileen. Don't forget to leave your banner with us, so we can get it up."

Eileen shook her head. "It's at the bottom of the box, lad. Don't look at me, it were my Jason that packed it."

Courtney sniggered. "He's a lazy get, how did you manage to get him up that early?"

"I told him there was a tenner in it," she said, making for the door. "But he'll be getting nowt now. Not with a soggy banner to show for it, the useless layabout."

"Well, thanks again. We'll make sure to tell everyone that you made them."

She waved back at them, already thinking about teacakes and gross margins.

"Ta-ra you two, all the hairy chest."

***

First through the door was Jaydon Morrison, a twenty-six year old computer programmer in a white hazmat suit.

"He looks like a professional," Courtney whispered to Pete. "He'll not feel a flake in that get up."

Pete directed Jaydon to his seat where the contestant closed his eyes and sunk into a deep meditation.

They heard Norman before they saw him.

"Annie, love, you're looking well. Is that a new gilet?"

Giggles wafted into the foyer from the street. "Are you taking part in the contest, Councillor Roach?"

"No love, I wouldn't want to embarrass them," he boomed, as his generous form filled the doorway. "Just here to support the troops."

A small, dark-haired woman pushed in from behind, her face flushed. "Pete? I'm Teresa Hibbert from the Chronicle. Just come from a family fun day, got you, then off to cover the rugby. When are you starting? Soon, yes?"

"Um."

Courtney zipped in front of Pete's thousand-yard stare. "We've got two more contestants due, shouldn't be long."

Teresa's shoulders slumped. "I've got seven events and my day is so finely timetabled I can only pee twice."

Pete raised his hand. "Would you like me to make you a cup of tea?"

Setting her camera bag onto a nearby seat, Teresa laughed. "Did you hear what I said about pee breaks? Go on then, a drop of milk and two sugars. RIP my bladder, eh?"

"He'll throw in a biscuit, won't you Pete?" Courtney asked, patting his retreating back.

Despite his rictus grin, Norman was incandescent. He'd never known such blatant disrespect. *Where's my cuppa? Where's my biscuit?*

Before he could deliver an invigoratingly funny yet heart-warming speech that nobody had asked for, another member of the great unwashed bumped into him.

"Excuse me, elected member here!" he joked, turning around.

"Didn't figure you'd need a free feed, Norman."

"Ernie Noble."

"In the flesh, as slender as it is."

Norman took in Ernie's shell suit and slippers. "Isn't sausage meat a bit rich for you? Considering you share meals with your pet rat?"

"How do you know Celeste doesn't like sausage rolls? Rats have rich tastes, as you'd know well."

***

Pete was developing a gnawing hunger. The sausage rolls smelled heavenly but were rapidly cooling. If Tanya Harris didn't hurry up, they'd only have two contestants. *I need a sausage roll dripping in vinegar and dipped in ketchup.*

"Courtney, can you interview Ernie, Jaydon and the dignitaries? Get some quotes about the library and take plenty of photos for our Facebook page?"

"Already on it," she said, snapping close-ups of Pete's furrowed brow. "You need to relax. There's loads of spectators and they're gobbling up Tina's muffins, happy as Larry. Even Vi's being nice. I swear I heard her tell the Mayor that the library saved her marriage. Dunno how that worked but I'm not asking."

Pete smiled. "You're hyper."

"Yeah, I'm loving this. And don't worry, I'll make sure everyone signs the petition before they leave," she promised, before diving back into the crowd.

Pete's watch showed that they were running eight minutes over and still no sign of the mysterious Tanya.

Is this happening?

———————— *** ————————

Behind plates of lukewarm sausage rolls, jugs of water and assorted condiments sat Jaydon, Ernie. And Pete.

The craft club had bagsied front row seats.

"You know it's very telling that three men are up there," Violet observed.

"What do you mean, Vi?" Mal asked politely.

"No intelligent woman would humiliate herself like that in public."

Tina, who was sitting in front guarding her buns, pretended not to have heard.

"Actually, Vi," Helen said smugly, "there was a woman taking part but she had to pull out."

Violet crossed her arms. "She obviously saw sense then, didn't she?"

"Well, according to my source, she fell outside Wetherspoons last night and sprained both her wrists."

"Just proves my point," Violet spat. "No decorum."

Tina looked innocently up at Helen. "Do you mean your Steph? Is she your source?"

"No decorum," Violet repeated.

***

Pete didn't care about getting a warning. He was saving the day. He was maybe saving the library. They had at least sixty spectators and Teresa the photographer had stuck around on the promise of a packet of Jammy Dodgers.

The only fly in the ointment was Councillor Roach who kept wandering off to look under bookshelves.

The Mayor approached the trio holding a large stopwatch. "Now then, you have five minutes to eat as many sausage rolls as you can. Please don't vomit on the carpet as the Council has informed me they've run out of spare tiles." She turned to the crowd for the inevitable laugh. "There are buckets for, you know, and jugs of water to ease your progress. May the best greedy guts win!"

And with that she started the clock.

Fortuitously, Pete hadn't had time for breakfast and was ravenously hungry.

That was his first mistake.

As much as Pete loved beige food, his stomach had never digested more than two sausage rolls in one sitting. For Pete, meat and pastry was best consumed on the move, not at a table with an audience.

***

Courtney only realised she'd been holding her breath when the Mayor asked her where the toilets were. She looked at her and blasted her face with hot air.

"Sorry, Mayor Mackay," she cried, as the woman screwed up her face. "I've been stress eating cheese and onion crisps."

The Mayor laughed it off. "I've smelled worse."

Courtney was lost for words and the feeling terrified her.

"Um, so, I was wondering where the little girl's room was?" She looked at her watch. "I need to be quick, eh?"

With her mouth firmly shut, Courtney pointed the mayor in the right direction.

As she turned to watch Pete cement his reputation as a Mad Pit legend, she caught Councillor Roach out of the corner of her eye. He was running his hands along the top shelf of the Local History display.

***

Pete was a mess.

His shirt was a canvas of pastry, water and grease. Three minutes in and he'd only managed four delicious sausage rolls, each one drowned in ketchup and a mountain of salt.

To add to his misery he knew that he was only seconds away from hating sausage rolls forever.

It was time for a spot of tough decision-making.

He held up his hand, pushed back his chair and dragged his carb-laden body to the toilet.

***

There were murmurs among the crowd that Jaydon was, in fact, an android as no living human could possibly consume that many sausage rolls that quickly.

Unblinking eyes fixed on the back wall, his arms pumped fatty pastry into his open mouth with no sign of slowing down.

With thirty seconds remaining, he inserted roll number eight.

***

Ernie was having the time of this life.

'Free sausage rolls from 'The La-al Teacake' was number six on his bucket list, before 'a kiss from Camilla Parker-Bowles' and after 'a bit part on The Archers as a fortune-telling vagrant.'

Ernie had no intention of winning.

He was here for the food.

————————— *** —————————

Between the table and the toilet Pete's stomach had twisted into a thousand complicated knots.

He silently prayed that Maeve had left a generous supply of loo roll and that Courtney was somewhere far, far away. Like Australia, or Barrow-in-Furness.

As he staggered forward, clutching his stomach, he watched the Mayor vacate the toilet and Councillor Roach enter it. *This is it. This is the story that people will tell their families. The story of my public downfall.*

Bile raced up his gullet and into his watering mouth. Without hesitation he dropped to his knees and vomited hot pastry and sausage meat over a fire extinguisher.

Wiping his mouth he looked up, relieved to find that everyone's attention was on the winner, Jaydon, who could barely raise a smile, the consummate professional robot that he was.

Pete willed Councillor Roach out of the loo, out of the building and out of all of their lives. Fearful of an encore, he raised a trembling hand.

Tap tap.

"I'm coming now! Just thoroughly washing my hands, as we all should."

Norman stormed out of the loo, a cotton bag clamped to his chest. His eyes darted to the vomit, then to Pete and then back to the vomit. "Aye lad, sausage rolls not agreeing with you?"

"Um, no. I need the, er, toilet," Pete stuttered, staring at his wet shoes.

"Go ahead. I've got to rush off, babies to attend and events to kiss."

Keeping his head down, Pete bolted for the toilet, briefly considering whether anyone would notice if he moved in to live out his life as a mute hermit.

***

Despite coming last, Ernie decided that he was runner-up. As far as he was concerned Pete hadn't been disqualified for leaving his seat mid-contest.

"Ernie and Jaydon, come over here for a photo!" Teresa roared. "The rugby club needs me to take lots of photos of muscled thighs and I'm not letting them down."

As Ernie cajoled the walking hazmat suit, his eyes lit upon Councillor Roach and his package making a swift Irish exit.

"Bugger."

Chapter Thirty Two

Ernie and his loaded belly traipsed to the only remaining public pay phone in Seatown to impart the bad news.

"Maeve, love?"

"Is that you, Ernie?"

"Yeah."

"Is that the fruit machine at Kelly's Taxi rank I can hear?"

"Yeah, I'm on the phone outside."

"What's up?"

"Well, I put the boat in a nice hiding place but now Cockroach has it."

"Why didn't you give it to Tristan? Where did you put it?"

"At the bottom of the babby's changing station in the library toilet. I couldn't find Tris, so I thought I'd make it fun for 'im, like a proper treasure hunt!"

"Says a lot about my cleaning if I didn't notice it. Flipping heck, Ernie."

"Sorry, lass. I should have just handed it to Tristan in the first place."

"Yes, that might have been the sensible thing to do. You were being very dramatic, weren't you?"

"Just a bit, eh?"

"So what should we do?"

"Don't worry, Maeve, I'll get it back."

"Listen to me Ernie, don't go breaking the law!"

"I'll try not to."

"Did you just belch?"

"Yeah, I've just eaten seven sausage rolls. Sorry, lass."

Chapter Thirty Three

Norman felt like the cat that got the clotted cream.

Fleeing the scene with his booty, he fixed his eyes to the ground and focused on reaching his car without fuss.

He *knew* this dinky boat was the answer; what other reason was there for it appearing in that rank toilet? Sometimes a lengthy bowel movement was all that was needed for some good old fashioned clarity. Thank God he'd had those day-old steak bakes for breakfast.

While Lesley's at yoga I'll use her eyebrow tweezers and take it apart, piece by piece. Then I'll go golfing.

Today wasn't the day to engage an old granny in conversation about NHS waiting times.

Varicose veins be damned, he had loftier ambitions than having his ear bent by poor people.

***

Norman pulled into his drive, admiring the immaculate lawn that, thanks to serious chemical intervention, housed no unnecessary animals or insects. Birds also avoided *The Treetops*; sparrows had long memories and the BB gun incident was still fresh.

He plucked the cotton bag from the passenger footwell and got out of the car. Lesley sprang from the front door sporting lime green yoga gear and wearing fuschia pink trainers. *How do I bring up that her wardrobe clashes with the house?*

"Just a quick stop, love, I'm meeting Geoff at the course in half an hour."

Lesley rolled her eyes. "You mean you're going straight to the nineteenth hole."

Planting a light kiss on her freshly made-up face, he headed for the front door. "Yes, I'm all about the pints, Les," he laughed nervously. "I'll bring my clubs for show in case I bump into a constituent."

"What have you got there?" she asked, shoving her kit into the boot of her mint green Fiat 500.

Norman hugged the bag to his chest. "Just a new hobby. Mini ship-in-a-bottle."

"I'm not quite sure how to respond to that information," she replied, studying her husband of eight years. "Don't wait up, I'm going to Janine's botox party after."

"Have fun, love," he said, stepping into the hallway. "Will you ask Janine to ring her mum?"

"I'll try but she'll be knee deep in crow's feet," Lesley sighed, sliding into the front seat. "Shoes, Norm!"

Norman kicked off his loafers and watched as she zipped out of the cul-de-sac, almost certainly breaking the twenty miles per hour speed limit.

He closed the front door and padded into the kitchen. Carefully placing the bag onto the worktop, he considered his next steps.

I'll just make a cuppa first.

As he switched on the kettle and removed a mug from the tree, his phone vibrated. Pulling it out of his trouser pocket, he looked at the screen and tutted: *Pauline Graves.*

"Hello, Pauline. You alright?" He looked in the cupboard for any kind of chocolate biscuit. It was bare. *Lesley's been purging again.*

"Councillor Roach, thank God you picked up," she breathed. "We need you."

Well, well, well.

"What's the emergency?" he asked, in his deepest voice.

He thought he heard laughing. *Nah.* "I've just had reports of illegal fishing down at the river. By the nature reserve. I knew you'd want to know."

"Those little rats! They're back, even after the last time?"

"Yes, Councillor. There's more of them, and they're drinking cider. Can you do something?"

Norman's face coloured. "What's happened to the noble sport of angling, Pauline? Can't the distinguished gent have nothing for himself?"

"It's a disgrace, that's what it is. I'd pack a lunch if I were you, Norman. They're scattered all over the bike path, tripping up people and whatnot. You could be there for a while."

Norman was in two minds. He looked at the bag. *I'll stash it somewhere.*

"Good idea, Pauline. I could bring my tackle too, make an afternoon of it. Who needs golf when you've got rainbow trout, eh?"

Pauline exhaled. "Norman, you're a lifesaver. Thank you."

"That's why I'm a politician, Pauline," he said, before hanging up.

He patted his bladder. *Too much weak library tea. I'll have a wee first, then I'll go.*

Pauline tossed her phone onto the sofa. "The tickling was uncalled for, Hazel."

235

"I couldn't help it. You looked so serious talking to the worst person on earth."

Pauline gave her a shove. "If you weren't my favourite cousin I'd put you in the famous Graves sleeper hold."

"I'm immune to that. Plus, we're both in our fifties."

The two women grew silent, taking a moment to ponder their very peculiar circumstances.

"Right, we're wasting time," Pauline said, hands on her hips. "You'd better ring Ernie and tell him he has a head start."

Hazel's face fell. "He doesn't have a phone."

"What?" Pauline exploded. "Did that not occur to you? You know Norman would take great pleasure hanging me out to dry, Hazel."

"We'll have to introduce a third party," Hazel decided, the colour returning to her cheeks. "Actually, Pauline, it's for the best, we can't trust Ernie not to get himself arrested again."

Shaking her head, Pauline opened the drinks cabinet and pulled out a bottle of brandy. Hazel frowned. "It's for the shock. Do you want one?"

***

A quick gulp of brandy and Hazel was commandeering Operation 'The King's Maiden' like a pro.

She pulled her phone from her handbag. "I can't believe my brain is this brainy, Pauline."

"Make the most of it while it lasts," Pauline laughed, refilling their glasses. "Who are you phoning?"

Hazel put her finger to her lips. "Sue? Yeah, it's Hazel. Can you do me a massive favour?"

Switching to speakerphone, Hazel set her device on Pauline's kitchen table.

"What's wrong, lass? I'm up to my elbows in bleach here."

"Maeve told me you clean Norman Roach's house. Is that right?"

"Yeah, for my sins. You know there's not a chocolate biscuit in that whole house. And her underwear drawer! It's obscene!"

Hazel was eyeing the fresh brandy. "Sue, we're in a pickle and we need the key to Norman's house. No-one will find out about this, your job will be safe."

Sue laughed. "I'm retiring to Torrevieja at the end of the year, that's how far away from Cockroach I want to be."

"So we can have it?"

"What do you need it for?"

Hazel felt full disclosure called for. "He stole something that belongs to Seatown."

There was the briefest of silences. "I'll meet you at the entrance to Seaview Gardens. I'll be wearing a tan trench coat and holding a copy of the Seatown Chronicle in my right hand. Upside down."

"Sue, I've known you for twenty years but if it gives you a thrill, go for it."

_____ *** _____

The Mercedes-Benz C-Class glided along the busy Seatown roads, its driver dutifully ignoring his environs, choosing instead to hide behind tinted windows and bask in Bach. Boys on bikes flew past. Rotting factories lay vacant. Elderly couples walked to the shops. Happy young couples pushed buggies.

Norman was bulging with righteous anger, ready to displace law-breakers with the mighty hand of the elected representative. No licence, no fishing. It was simple; there could be no place for confusion.

Swinging into Derwent Avenue, he peered over the steering wheel towards the nature reserve main entrance.

Everything looked suspiciously quiet.

_____ *** _____

Ernie's head shuddered against the bus window. The irritating vibration kept him focused on the task at hand. It had been a few years since his last break-in and he was worried. Norman's crib was in a cul-de-sac and cul-de-sacs had eyes. Dozens of curious eyes.

He looked down at his outfit. Would it be convincing?

He'd purchased the Postman Pat costume from 'The Children's Society', on a whim. He sometimes felt like splurging on fancy clothing after a Dynasty binge. He'd bought that video box set from 'The Children's Society' too.

At his stop Ernie got up, stepped over Roy, the number twenty one drunk, and alighted the bus.

***

Hazel and Sue met by the Seaview Gardens sign.

"Where's your trench coat?" Hazel asked, a little disappointed that Sue had turned up wearing a pair of grey jogging bottoms and a lemon yellow hoodie.

"I didn't want it to clash with your red one," she laughed, handing over the key.

"It's my signature look, Sue. Go red or go home."

Sue leaned in and whispered. "We're being very naughty, you know."

"It'll be worth it, I promise," Hazel assured her. "Listen, do you use the library?"

"Only to print stuff, love," Sue said, shaking a bug out of her short black bob.

"Can you use it some more? And your family? It's going to close otherwise."

Sue nodded. "All hands on deck, eh?"

"It's the beating heart of our town," Hazel admitted. "And it needs some serious CPR."

Sue raised her eyebrows. "So does that mean the 'Drunken Sailor' is the liver?"

Hazel left Sue to her weekly shop and walked with purpose towards Norman's well kept bungalow.

She fingered the key in her pocket, conscious that her hands were clammy. *Look at the pretty gardenias. Isn't this a nice cul-de-sac? Nothing to see here, I'm just a well-off woman visiting her rich friend. Stop thinking, Hazel, you look insane.*

A woman brandishing a spotlessly clean trowel gazed at Hazel. Kneeling on a gardening mat and sporting a floral floppy hat, she tracked Hazel's every step.

I'd look more convincing if I was carrying a bucket and mop. Why didn't I think of that?

Fighting the urge to gallop, she casually approached Norman's home.

A flash of blue disappeared behind the garage.

What the…?

With trembling fingers, Hazel removed the key from her pocket and opened the front door. She knew Lesley was at yoga; the woman never missed an excuse to don head to toe lycra, and there'd been talk she was heading straight to Janine's botox party afterwards.

In a dark corner of her mind bloomed a faint glow of confidence that this would be an in and out operation. But that dim light was extinguished at the thought of humiliating her family by getting arrested. *I'm the substitute cleaner, officer. Sue's sick, officer. I forgot my cleaning gear, officer. Here, I'll put on the handcuffs myself, officer. Save you a job.*

Closing the door behind her she tiptoed through the hall and into the kitchen, taking in the abandoned mug and open cupboard. The kettle was still warm and an unpleasantly strong whiff of *Lynx Africa* lingered. The walls were crowded with 'Live, Laugh, Love' plaques in a dozen different fonts and the glossy white kitchen units were, incredibly, smudge-free. *Do they wear latex gloves?*

"Focus, Hazel," she muttered, looking around the kitchen. "Where would Norman put the boat?"

Before she could venture further, there was a crash.

Hazel flinched. "Flipping heck!"

The connecting door to the garage rumbled. Feeling reckless, Hazel crept towards the door and opened it.

And Postman Pat came tumbling out.

***

"I've got a parcel for you, lass," Ernie laughed, as he lay on his back, covered in grit. "Have you seen my cat, Jess? I think she's done a runner."

Hazel picked him up and brushed him off. "Are you concussed?"

"Nah, I fall all the time. It does me good," he said, straightening his uniform. "What are you doing here?"

"Same as you, I reckon. How on earth did you get in?"

Ernie pointed to the narrow garage window and then to his slender frame. "It were open a smidge so I squeezed in."

Hazel looked with dismay at the disassembled shelving, paint cans and tools strewn across the garage floor. "You'll be covered in bruises! Did anyone see you?"

"It's Saturday afternoon, Hazza. All these rich gadgies will be at the golf course and the wives will be meeting their toy boys at the gym."

Hazel was worried; he was only partially right. "All apart from that woman gardening. She's a witness."

"I know Glenda, she's drunk most of the time," Ernie assured her. "If the filth asks her anything, she'll not remember."

"Who drinks and gardens?" Hazel asked him, as she poked into empty pots and cardboard boxes. "Where is this bloody boat?"

"Look at me, I'm a ballerina!" Ernie squawked, gyrating with a black tutu hanging from his hips. A cymbal clattered to the floor. "Bugger, he's got a drum kit and all."

Hazel hauled Ernie out of the garage and into the kitchen. "Right, I'm giving us sixty seconds to find the boat. So get moving."

"Yessir."

The duo ransacked as politely as they could, making sure every inspirational knickknack was left exactly as they had found it.

"Forty-five, forty-four, forty-three…"

Ernie was bent over the umbrella stand. "Counting down isn't helping, Hazel."

"Forty-two!" she shouted, running into the living room. "Get a move on, Pat, or I'll have Jess skinned and served on a plate!"

***

Norman was confused.

The riverbank was a picture of serenity. Dawdling lovers held hands, old gents gathered on benches and every dog was on a lead.

I smell politicking.

He approached the nearest bench where three octogenarians sat drinking tea from thermos flasks. One of them had an opened packet of custard creams on their lap.

"Gentlemen, how are you? Loving life, I hope?"

The ringleader, an eighty three year-old called Bill, piped up. "Every minute of it, Councillor. What brings you down here on a Saturday. Isn't Sunday your day?"

Norman *harrumphed*. "I've just received a report of illegal fishing and drinking. Have you come across anything at odds with the law today?

"Other than Marco's bad breath here and a gang of grey squirrels, not a thing."

"I thought as much," Norman admitted. "Thank you boys, enjoy your afternoon."

Norman turned on his heel and dashed off.

The three men watched him go. "Norm's in a hurry, lads. Watch him saunter up that path, like a snail out of hell."

_____ *** _____

"I've found it, Hazza!"

Hazel followed the sound of Ernie's voice to the downstair's loo. The man stood triumphantly, tightly gripping the bag just in case it fell into the toilet.

"Well done, Ern."

"It's ironic really, considering I left it in a toilet in the first place. Eh, Hazel?"

Hazel beckoned for Ernie to pass her the bag. "Very poetic, Ernie."

"My ears are pricking, Hazza."

"Excuse me, young man?"

Ernie held up his hand and closed his eyes. "Quiet, woman."

Hazel walked towards the front door and risked a quick peek out of the glass side panel.

"I can't see anything."

"I can hear summat," Ernie whispered, his face paling. "It's that galoot's ozone destroyer."

"Let's make like a tree and leave, Ern," Hazel laughed, grabbing the man's arm and making for the back door.

"We can't leave the back door open! He'll know we were here!"

Hazel shoved the bag inside her coat and buttoned it up. "Ernie, the boat's gone, he'll know *someone* was here."

"Spot on, lass," Ernie said, his brain catching up. "We've stolen what *he* stole from us and there's nothing he can do about it."

"Come on, get going!" Hazel screeched, sweat trickling down the sides of her face. She held the door open for him, then carefully shut it after he landed on the sandstone patio.

The dynamic duo sped across Norman's perfect lawn and crouched by his tidy conifers.

"We'll wait until he's gone inside and then scoot off on our hunkers," Hazel whispered. "Can you manage that, Postman Pat?"

Ernie nodded. "This is the best Saturday I've had all week."

***

Norman barreled his car into the driveway. *God help me if I've left scorch marks.*

Disregarding his reputation in the cul-de-sac as a steady pair of hands, he left his car door swinging in the breeze in an attempt to get into his house three seconds faster.

He paused outside of the downstair's loo, readying himself for what he knew was to come.

Opening the door, all he found was a well-thumbed copy of *Today's Angler* and the empty spot where his boat should have been.

———————— *** ————————

As Glenda dropped her trowel and teetered into the kitchen for a fresh gin and tonic, a high pitched scream erupted from number ten. *That Lesley needs to learn some neighbourly boundaries.*

Chapter Thirty Four

Sunday morning found Janet buried under her duvet re-reading Pete's excessively long text message drama about the Mad Pit Sausage Roll Massacre.

She'd never laughed so hard on a weekend morning in an empty bed. Poor Pete. Thank God no one but Cockroach had caught his puke sideshow. He'd even cleaned it up afterwards, having begged Sam the butcher for a bucket of sawdust.

She was proud of the lad; he'd done well to bring the Pit some much needed publicity, and he did it all himself, with a little help from Courtney who, according to Pete, had been high as a kite in the presence of the 'paparazzi.' Courtney had allegedly reported heart palpitations and 'tingly fingers', such was her excitement.

Stretching in her warm cocoon, her foot nudged a soft, snoozing lump.

"Time for a bacon butty and a big mug of sugary coffee, Sparky. Then we'll go for a walk."

_____ *** _____

Courtney's thumbs ached.

She'd spent Saturday night hunched over her phone creating *Save Our Library* social media posts and threatening friends and family with public humiliation if they didn't share every last one.

She'd posted twenty-four photos, in all. Tempted as she was to publicise Pete's humiliating vomit spectacle, she'd decided against it. The last thing Pete needed was to know that she'd captured every last string of sausage roll spit on her smartphone.

Courtney reached for her phone, a smile spreading across her face. "Yeah, baby!"

The notifications were rolling in.

"They can't close the Mad Pit! I've been a member since I was a nipper!"

"Where will I print my family fotos if the library closes?"

"I love going 2 the parent & toddler group. If I got preggers again, do you think they'd keep it open?"

"Nice photos, Court. Who's that cutie in the shirt and tie? Is he single?"

"There goes another public building. What's happening to our proud town?"

"Is this you @Jaydog? I'm surprised the grease didn't fry your circuits."

Her bedroom door shuddered.

"Court, can you make me some cereal? I'm starving!"

"Make it yourself, Nathan!" she yelled. "Where's mam?"

Nathan continued banging. "Collecting her Avon from Aunty Marie. Can I come in, please?"

Courtney dropped her phone onto the duvet.

"When did you learn manners, you little squirt?"

"From the telly."

"Come on then."

Her little brother opened the door and shuffled in, sporting messy hair and a worn pair of Spongebob Squarepants pyjamas. "You slapped me on the back of the head the last time I walked in, Court. It's called self-preservation."

Courtney smirked. "You've been reading far too many books."

"Yeah, from your precious library," he laughed, rubbing the sleep from his eyes. "You think they'll keep it open now that you've had your contest?"

His sister pulled a thick pink dressing gown from the foot of her bed and put it on. "Probably not. Come on, I'll show you how to 'make cereal', you lazy little bugger."

***

"Tell me you're joking, Tristan!" Lupin squealed into the phone, head resting on a plump purple cushion, legs dangling over the side of the sofa. Her cat leapt from its warm spot, landed on the lid of her record player and skittered into the kitchen, tail between its legs. "Oops, I've scared the puss. Anyway, what else did Courtney tell you?"

"That he ran down to the butcher's and asked old Sam for some sawdust."

Lupin grimaced. "Do we have any spare carpet tiles? It's going to stink in there tomorrow."

"Violet will go off on one," Tristan sighed. "We can nick a few tiles from the computer room."

Lupin scratched her scalp. *I need to wash my hair.* "Good idea," she said, swinging her legs off the couch and padding to the bathroom. "But we need another stunt."

"Yes, we do," Tristan sighed. "Why is keeping a library open so hard?"

"You're a ragged trousered philanthropist, Tristan," Lupin drawled, as she turned on the shower. "This is your arena."

Chapter Thirty Five

"I loooove cleaning up vomit, I loooove cleaning up vomit," Maeve warbled, dipping her scrubbing brush into a bucket of hot, soapy water.

He did a pretty decent job of cleaning up the chunks, but the smell! She gagged. *I'm going to be sick.*

Maeve had been scraping up vomit for years, but in grotty pub toilets, not libraries. Apart from the parent and toddler mass spewing incident of twenty-thirteen, the worst Maeve had to clean was Ernie's errant piddle. She leaned into the scrubbing motion and watched with satisfaction as the thin film of grease disappeared.

They'll end up swapping this one for a computer room tile.

A few feet away,'The King's Maiden' peeked out of its comfortable cotton bag.

But before she could head upstairs to Janet's office, Maeve had to wipe down the fire extinguisher.

Chapter Thirty Six

The quartet talked over a large, steaming pot of tea.

Janet noticed with distaste that the cream kitchen cupboards were slick with condensation. *Yuck, does that always happen?*

"From now on we're swapping tea for cold drinks. This kitchen is damper than Ernie's y-fronts."

Pete paled. "What?"

Janet winked. "It's a health and safety hazard."

"She's joking, Pete," Lupin said, spooning sugar into her mug. "You look as white as a sheet. Do you feel sick?"

"Ooh, low blow," Tristan laughed. He gazed at Pete's mortified face. "She'd make you puke, eh?"

Pete stared at his mug. "Well, what have *you* three done to keep this place open?"

To say the ensuing silence was uncomfortable would have been an understatement.

"Look! Biscuits!" Janet pulled a packet of chocolate hobnobs from her bag and proffered them to Pete.

Before Pete could accept the peace offering, Lupin stood up. "You know what, Pete? Let's go and consult the public." She opened the kitchen door and beckoned her colleagues to follow.

***

The craft club had a new member and no one quite knew what to make of it.

As their de facto leader, Violet took it upon herself to greet the incomer. "So, um. You're Dennis?"

A man in his late twenties beamed up at Violet from his seat. He wore a faded Metallica t-shirt, black jeans and battered Converse sneakers. "Hi everyone, I'm Dennis but my friends call me Deadeye."

Nobody spoke.

"Don't ask, ha ha!"

Malcolm was noticeably torn. One one hand, it was nice to have another man in the group, but on the other, this fella was competition. So, Malcolm stretched out his hand in welcome. "I'm Mal."

"Mal," Tina tittered, as she watched the two men shake hands. "What's your specialty, um, Deadeye?"

Dennis looked chuffed. "Great question, er...?"

"Tina."

"Hi, Tina. Yes, I would say cross-stitch? But then I'm also very partial to fluid art of an evening."

Violet's heart melted. "Oh, Deadeye, I'd love to see a bit of your fluid art."

"I've heard it all now, Vi," Helen snapped. "Dennis, welcome to the team. Don't mind Vi, she's happily married."

Tina set her tupperware on top of the table and removed the lid. "Cupcake, Deadeye?"

***

"Here we go, another new member," Janet sighed, reapplying *Cerise Haze* on the move. "How long do you think this one will last?"

Tristan, Lupin and Pete followed their manager to the craft corner. "He looks far too enthusiastic," Tristan commented, watching Dennis tuck into a lemon drizzle cupcake. "Vi will have that knocked out of him in no time."

"Bugger," Janet moaned, pulling out her phone and looking at it. "I've just vibrated. It's a reminder that I've a conference call at half ten. Lupin, you can handle this can't you?"

"Course I can, boss." Lupin swaggered ahead, talking over her shoulder. "In ten minutes we'll have a library-saving idea and then everyone will be happy."

"Was she being sarcastic?" Janet asked Pete, giving him a smile and a nudge. "Sorry I offended you earlier, love. You did a fantastic job on Saturday."

"Thanks, Janet," Pete smiled. "And yeah, she was."

Janet rushed to her office, as keen to attend an operations meeting as Violet was to openly admire Helen's jewelry.

Lupin approached the craft table and laid her hand on Violet's shoulder. "Vi, hello! Are you going to introduce us to your new member?"

Violet turned in her seat to look up at Lupin. "Lupin, love, you look a bit twitchy. Are you alright?"

"Never better. I really love living on my nerves," Lupin replied, staring into Violet's eyes. "So, considering you all love the library so much, how are you going to keep us open? Vi, you start."

Violet looked at Dennis and laughed nervously. "Well, Lupin, we've been having meetings about it. In my house. And we've got Dennis now, too."

Dennis' gaze was fixed on his left hand.

Lupin crouched down beside Violet. "And what ideas did you have?" she asked, clapping her hands. "We need solid ideas!"

Tristan reached over everyone's heads and lifted up Tina's tupperware box. "How about we all enjoy one of Tina's delicious cupcakes? Lupin? Are you ready to transform back into a normal person?"

Nobody spoke.

Malcolm coughed. "Actually, I had an idea."

Lupin dashed to the other side of the table and hugged Malcolm's head to her stomach. "Mal, you'd better not let us down."

As Lupin's eyes bored into Malcolm's soul, Tristan passed the cupcakes around.

"Well, don't get too excited," Malcolm started, talking to Lupin's navel. "But we were planning on holding an awareness-raising tea dance in the care home I work at. Invite important people, get them onside."

Lupin continued to squeeze Malcolm's skull. "Yes, go on."

"I can't really breathe, Lupin."

"We're right at the window, love," Helen pointed out. "People will think you're assaulting a member of the public."

Lupin released Malcolm and jumped back onto Pete's foot. "Sorry, Malcolm. Oh, sorry Pete."

"Anyway," Malcolm continued. "My boss, Louise, has just had to cancel it because the insurers won't allow more than fifty people in the ballroom."

Violet actually growled. "For crying out loud, Malcolm! This isn't helping my blood pressure. And Helen's face is so pale it's clashing with her Ready Brek muumuu."

"Vi," Helen cried. "It's an outdoor kaftan, not a muumuu."

"It's a two-man tent the colour of gruel, is what it is!"

Dennis was looking at the bus timetable on his phone.

Malcolm stood up and held out his arms. "Oh my God, we are so stupid. We should be having it here!"

"Even if we did, Mal," Tristan said, "how much awareness do you think a little tea dance is going to raise?"

Lupin nodded. "He's right. We need actual money, not just people's attention." She glanced at Pete's belly. "Could you and your friends spare a kidney each?"

Pete shook his head and backed away. "I'd better go," he said, giving the thumbs up. "There's someone at reception."

"Pensioners are very tenacious and they'll fight if we ask them to fight. Don't forget how many of them are bussed in here every Tuesday morning to borrow their romances and westerns," Malcolm continued, warming to his monologue. "Anyway, Eileen's going to do the sarnies and cakes, and Sam offered to fetch in a hog roast."

Helen scoffed. "Pulled pork? How modern."

"And we can invite elected members, the press, the mayor…"

"…and Father Christmas," Violet spat, still annoyed that this hadn't been her idea.

Tristan offered Violet a knowing smile. "Each one of you will be equally responsible for all of the ways this will go wrong."

"Can we hold it here, then?" Malcolm asked. "We promise to sweep up every crumb and turf out any rowdy pensioners."

Tristan looked unconvinced. "When were you thinking?"

Malcolm sank back into his seat. "Friday evening?"

"That's not giving us much time to get organised, Mal," Tristan moaned. "Can't it be put back?"

"You don't know the old folks, Tristan," Malcolm complained. "They were so upset when we had to cancel, so I told them we'd keep the date and find a new venue. Anyway, it's better here, isn't it? In the actual place we're trying to save?"

Dennis cleared his throat. "This is a library. How on earth can you hold a tea dance in a library?"

Violet was disappointed at the new man's lack of foresight. "If they can invite people to come here and choke down sausage rolls, they can clear the floor for a naff rendition of 'Chantilly Lace."

"My dad knows a band that could play," Lupin suggested, warming up to the idea. "Do you need one, Mal?"

"Well, I was just going to make a Spotify playlist," Malcolm admitted. "So, yes, that would be great, Lupin. Thank you."

"If I'd known we weren't doing watercolours, I'd have fetched my flipchart," Violet cried. "Dennis, take notes!"

Dennis sighed and picked up a biro.

***

Janet opened her office door and immediately tripped over a stuffed giraffe. She picked up the offending animal and placed it on a shelf. "I love that my office isn't an office at all."

"And who are you?" she asked the white cotton bag that sat by her computer. "Another one of Lupin's lost family learning packs?"

Settling into her chair, Janet lifted the bag, fully expecting it to house grubby picture books. Upon inspection, she discovered a delicate model ship bearing the inscription, 'The King's Maiden."

"Oh. Oh! OH!"

***

A nervous-looking Ernie had joined the extended group. He sat perched on the edge of a children's chair, his eyes level with Violet's bust.

"Alright, marra?" he asked Dennis, smoothing his hair with trembling hands. "You know I'm only an honorary member of this club on account that I don't do any crafts when I'm here."

Dennis continued writing, conscious that Violet was still firing suggestions into his ear. "Is that right?"

"He's a pain in the aspidistra," Tristan complained. "But he's our pain in the aspidistra."

Lupin scrutinised Ernie's facial expression. She'd recently done a Wowcher course on face reading and was confident that Ernie had either recently committed a crime or was mid-heart attack. "Are you alright, Ernie? You look shiftier than usual. No offence."

Ernie laughed but his eyes were troubled. "Ah, none taken, lass."

Janet materialised by his side, making him jump in his seat.

"Ernie Noble, you look like you'd know something about this, since you're so keen on stuff in bags."

She parked the bag on the table.

Dennis looked utterly baffled.

"Nah, I prefer bin bags," Ernie said, staring at his feet. "What is it? Don't keep us in suspenders."

Janet removed the boat and held it aloft. "It says 'The King's Maiden' on the side, Tristan."

Tristan was gobsmacked. "The boat. That's the boat! Is that the boat?"

The craft club gaped at the model, each of them wondering what on earth a boat had to do with anything, but welcoming the distraction from Violet's checklist.

"What boat?" Lupin asked, feeling like she was missing something significant.

Tristan reached over and reverently took the Maiden from Janet's hands. "The boat that was mentioned in the old minutes. Remember? 'The heinous vessel, 'The King's Maiden,' and its ill-gotten gains shall dwell by Cutter's Lane' boat?"

Pete had been standing behind Tristan, quietly calculating how many tables and chairs would fit on the ground floor and baulking at the obscene quantities of tea a clutch of dancing pensioners would demand. "That boat looks familiar."

"What?" Tristan whirled round to face Pete, holding the boat above his head.

"Yeah, it was high up," Pete confirmed.

"What are you talking about, lad?" Janet asked him.

Ernie chuckled and pointed towards the street outside. "He knows where she's been. Can't you remember, Janet? You spend enough time there sucking up those nasty blue cocktails."

Lupin clapped her hands. "The 'Drunken Sailor'! She's been there the whole time!"

"Look at you, calling a boat 'she'," Tristan mocked. "Not very feminist of you, Lup."

"Shurrup, loser," she laughed. "So, how's this supposed to help us?"

Tristan marvelled at the boat's detail. "Fascinating. I'll take it home and find out what I can. That alright, boss?"

Janet nodded. "Go for it, but be careful."

"What if it's haunted?" Dennis asked, excited at this turn of events. "Possessed by the spirit of Blackbeard!"

Helen patted Dennis on the hand. "Oh love, you don't believe in all that nonsense, do you?"

"Leave him alone, Helen," Tina scolded, maintaining eye contact with Dennis. "'There are more things in heaven and earth, Horatio, than are dreamt of in your philosophy.'"

Helen rolled her eyes. "What's got into you, Tina? You're normally a timid little mouse."

"I'm, uh, going to miss my bus," Dennis said. "I'd better get a move on."

Violet pulled the notebook from Dennis' grasp and continued making notes. "Haunted boats. Honestly. We have a tea dance to organise!"

Helen and Tina watched Dennis slip out of the huddle and make for the door.

"There's another one won't be back," Ernie cackled.

Chapter Thirty Seven

Just as Tristan was removing his lasagne from the microwave, the doorbell rang.

"Perfect timing," he groaned, dropping the molten hot container onto the kitchen worktop. A splash of bechamel sauce coated his hand. "Bugger!"

Behind the door was Lupin, holding a bag of sugary jam doughnuts.

"I knew you'd call," Tristan said. "I've not started my mains yet. Have you eaten?"

"Sorry, and yes." She shed her coat and dropped it onto an armchair that was covered with other coats. "I see you're still decorating. Have you picked a theme yet?"

He ripped the film from his lasagne and tipped the gluey mess onto a dinner plate. "Probation hostel, circa. 1985."

She nodded. "It works."

They both took a seat at Tristan's breakfast bar. "Keep those doughnuts handy," he asked, before dunking a fork into his dinner. "It'll only take a minute to eat half of this before I realise it's disgusting. I'll still be hungry."

"In that case I'll put the kettle on in preparation." Lupin got up to make tea. "Do you have decaf?"

"Do I have decaf? You may as well ask me if I prefer American beer. No, I do not have decaf."

Lupin tutted. "There goes my good night's sleep."

"I'm rock and roll, Lupin. Normal tea for me, even after six o'clock."

***

"I can guess why you're here," Tristan said, as he scraped the remnants of his lasagne into the bin.

Lupin drained her cuppa. "I just need to know how much my family was involved in this." She shook her head and blinked. "God, I wish I'd fetched some camomile bags over. I can already feel the caffeine lighting up all of my brain circuits."

Tristan padded into his home office, Lupin following with a plate of doughnuts. "Boat before doughnuts," he said. "Janet won't appreciate sticky fingerprints."

The boat sat on his desk, surrounded by towering piles of folded maps and county records. "It looks happy here," Lupin commented. "Not having to listen to Alan mangle the pub quiz, or breathe in stale beer fumes. I'm surprised it's still in such good nick."

"It is very clean. Someone's given it a makeover."

They stood over it, unsure what to do next.

266

"Maybe there's something inside." Tristan picked up a set of tweezers and pulled open a small door that revealed the interior of the ship's hold.

Lupin got down on her knees and peered inside. "Put your phone torch on, Tristan."

He handed her the phone.

"There's paper in here!"

Tristan handed her the tweezers. "Be careful, Lup, it might be ancient. Do you want me to do it?"

Lupin shook her head. "My hands are smaller than your shovels. Don't worry, I'll be careful."

***

"Well, now," Tristan said.

Lupin smiled. "Indeed."

"Are you happy?"

"Pretty much."

"What's up?"

"Well, it's nice to know that not every Lawson was a crook. So, yes, I am happy."

"Do you want a doughnut?"

"Is the bear Catholic?"

"We all eat too much sugar."

"Aye."

Chapter Thirty Eight

The remainder of the week was a whirl of strategic event management, (Violet's words) and catering for geriatrics, (Ernie's). Malcolm and his boss Louise booked a bus at a slashed rate, to ferry partygoers to the dance. Tina and Helen utilised their womanly wiles, (Helen's words) to invite key stakeholders and bring the local press on board.

Janet had successfully sweet-talked Amanda into allowing them to transform the library into a social club for flirtatious Sheltering Oaks residents.

Pete and Courtney just enjoyed being needed. Pete, following the success of his sausage roll eating contest, was tasked with begging local producers for free food and drink. Courtney, the Mad Pit's customer service champion, played bad cop, making retailers feel guilty for not offering Pete free food and drink.

With Janet's approval, Tristan and Lupin were holding their cards close to their respective chests.

***

"There's been a marked increase in visitors this last month," Janet told Amanda Love and Pauline Graves, passing them her report. "We have eighty-seven new registered users and we've added another two mental health first-aid training programmes. Plus, our children's reading challenges are proving very popular."

The three women sat around a circular meeting table, cradling cups of cold coffee and ignoring the, frankly sub-par, biscuits.

"Take a breath, Janet," Pauline smiled. "We've got it all here in front of us."

"Sorry, I'm very nervous. So not like me," Janet admitted.

Amanda was conflicted. She really didn't like Janet, with her big hair, full lips and 'I do it for the people' girl guide attitude. But every non-existent hair on Amanda's waxed body hated Norman Roach and his cabal of chauvinists. She swung her mane for a reassuring whiff of expensive shampoo. *I'll always have better hair.*

Pauline cleared her throat. "Janet, we're all happy that things have picked up. But we're on a deadline. Seatown needs money, it's as simple as that. And if the council can sell off an asset, that will be money for children's services."

"Now, Pauline," Amanda started. "As much as Janet and I don't see eye to eye, we all know who has plans for that plot."

Janet looked at the floor. *Amanda has clearly given up on job security.*

"I know, I shouldn't say it out loud," Amanda continued, "but he's convinced he'll get that plot for a song."

"Amanda, it's a conflict of interest," Pauline explained, pointing to a copy of the Elected Member Handbook. "No one can profit on a local authority asset as an elected member."

To her disgust, Amanda looked to Janet for backup.

"I think Amanda may have a point," Janet said. "There has been talk that he plans on buying the plot for his daughter."

Pauline leaned forward. "And where did you hear that, Janet?"

"Well, just general tittle tattle."

"Seriously? That's what we have to go on? Tittle tattle?"

Amanda stood up and refilled her mug from the urn. Tepid grey liquid spluttered out, landing everywhere but inside her cup. "For crying out loud. Anyone else want a top up of whatever this is?"

Pauline and Janet declined.

"Look, Janet," Pauline whispered. "I wouldn't trust Councillor Roach as far as I could throw him and I know he's buying up Seatown. But he's an outlier. An exception."

Amanda noticed Janet searching in her handbag. *Here comes the lippie.*

"He might be a lone wolf but he's still a threat," Janet warned, applying a fresh layer of *Letterbox Red*. "He'll stop at nothing to please that harpy daughter of his. And we all know how good politicians like him are at going through back doors to get what they want. I've no doubt he has links to local property developers."

Pauline picked up a biscuit, bit into it and scowled. "Government cuts equals crap biscuits."

"What should we do, Pauline?" Janet asked.

"Let your users continue with their efforts. That's their right, after all," she said, getting to her feet. "And I'll see what I can do about the roach infestation."

Ian couldn't believe what he was doing. Caddying for a bent politician when he should have been pulling up community centre managers for not maintaining their smoke alarms. *I'm doing it for Tyler.*

He watched Norman strut around the links like an ageing peacock, chatting up other balding peacocks. He'd actually slapped someone's back. One funny handshake and he'd be a step closer to sitcom villain status.

Ian plodded along the fairway to meet Norman at the eighth hole. "So, er, Councillor Roach?" Ian asked. "About that job for my Tyler?"

"Hush, lad," he chided. "I'm concentrating."

Norman putted the ball and missed. "That was your fault."

"Why am I here?" Ian hissed. "Does that job even exist?"

Without checking for witnesses, Norman gently tapped his ball into the hole. "No, Councillor Thomson caught on to what we were doing so it's being advertised."

"What?" Ian toppled Norman's golf bag onto the green. A six pack of pilsner rolled out.

Norman shielded the offending alcohol with his two-tone wingtip golf shoes. "Put that back in, stupid!"

"No, I will not!" Ian yelled. "I have actual work to be doing, Norman. And I saw you steal that hole."

"Alright lad, don't have a hissy fit," Norman seethed, saluting two approaching golfers. "Greg, Alan. Taking a break from being the kings of Cumbrian dairy?"

Ian knelt down to pick up the cans. "Tyler needs a job, Norman. He's not a well lad and you promised me you'd help him."

"I promise people a lot of things," Norman said out of the corner of his mouth, continuing to wave.

"Well then, let's tell your fake pals all about your beer and blatant cheating, shall we?" Ian huffed, dropping the cans back onto the grass.

"Listen, Ian," Norman whispered. "Janine will be opening a new salon soon and there'll be a maintenance job for Tyler. I'm sure he can wait a year, yeah? I hear there's a benefits increase coming soon, so that'll keep him in video games 'til then."

Ian wanted to seize Norman's putter and smash his skull with it.

"What are you smirking at?" Norman asked. "Can Tyler wait?"

"Yes, Councillor Roach, he can wait."

Chapter Thirty Nine

Courtney was admiring Pete's back.

"Courtney love, your eyes are on stalks," Helen laughed. "Shall we move this trestle table before Vi has a nervous breakdown?"

"Er, yeah," she said. "Sorry."

Pete shoved the sci-fi shelf against the wall. "Is she watching?"

"Yeah, mate," Tristan insisted. "She's either hypnotised by your raw masculinity or Helen's talking about clothes and boring the life out of her."

"Maybe I should push up my shirt sleeves. Apparently women like forearms."

Tristan looked at Pete's arms. "Yeah, not your forearms, lad. They're not veiny enough."

Pete dropped to the floor and pretended to tie his shoelace. "Vi's coming."

"Gentlemen, we're on the clock here," Violet scolded, holding up her clipboard. "The dance starts in two hours and we've still got to put up the bunting and arrange the tables and chairs for optimum dancing."

"We're on it, boss," Tristan said, flexing his bicep. "We'll have a clear floor in t-minus ten minutes."

"Oh, Tristan," Violet giggled, sweeping across the floor with a clipboard in one hand and a catering bag of PG-Tips in the other.

A gust of wind chilled the back of Violet's legs. "Sorry, we're closed for a major event!"

Ernie dropped a large chest onto the floor. "I'm your warm-up DJ. Help me with my LPs."

Violet was afraid to turn around. But she was pushed for time. "Ernie? What in the name of Saint Jude are you wearing?"

Ernie had torn apart eight separate charity shops and a jumble sale to look like the oldest member of the Village People, leading him to miss valuable telly time. *And who is she to talk? She's wearing a leopard print maxi dress with cream espadrilles. This isn't Benidorm! I'm getting out of these pleather hotpants, my gear's sweating.*

Violet fixed her eyes on the exit sign above the front door. "What on earth are you wearing, Ernie? We don't have a record player and there's only room for the band."

"Ha, well, Lupin has loaned me hers. And I'm setting up outside the kitchen."

Ernie pushed the box of vinyl along the floor with his biker booted feet. "Get ready to rock to Patsy Cline and smooch to The Ramones!"

276

Malcolm gripped Louise's wrist and pulled her onto the bus. "Yeah, I've got short legs," she giggled. "Live with it."

Louise turned to face the residents. "Right, ladies and gents, listen up. Following the ten-pin bowling incident I've been forced to mandate an outdoor events policy."

Elsie's hand shot up. "If Jim fell over, it was his own fault! The man's got vertigo!"

"You felt me up," Jim accused. "Just as I was taking my shot. There's a time and a place, Elsie. I could have had a strike!"

"Fair enough, Jim. I'll keep that in mind," Elsie agreed, winking. "Just watch your back on the dance floor, if you know what I mean."

Malcolm sank into his seat. "This is going to be a nightmare."

Louise clapped her hands. "Keep your mitts to yourselves or there'll be no bingo between now and Christmas."

The bus erupted into chaos.

***

"Seatown's answer to Diane Arbus coming through!" Teresa bumped open the front door with her backside and immediately started shooting.

"Always the professional, Teresa," Janet shouted over the heads of jiving couples. "Ernie's wearing lederhosen so avoid him, otherwise they'll shut us sooner."

"Duly noted," she said, pointing her camera at Janet's face.

"Oi! My hair's a mess, Teresa," Janet groaned, patting down her locks.

"Too late, love. I'm off to find Ernie."

***

Ernie sidled up to Teresa. "You missed me, lass."

Teresa looked him up and down. "I most definitely did not."

"No, my set. It was, what's the word, *eclectic*." He pulled out a small hip flask and drained what was left of his raspberry gin and tonic.

Teresa continued to snap. Reverend Nixon and his band of merry parishioners were collecting petition signatures. By the kitchen, Pete and Courtney were doling out tea, coffee and cakes to sweaty dancers, Tristan and Lupin were cosying up to the VIP guests and Councillor Roach was loitering by the toilet with a face like thunder. All to the tune of "Suspicious Minds."

"What's up with Roach?"

Ernie belched. "Sorry, lass. Shrek there wants to shut us down."

"Really? Why?" Teresa asked, pretending to act surprised that a known dodgy politician wanted to do something dodgy.

"Well," Ernie muttered, falling against a table of dirty cups and saucers. "Oops. Ernie. No, that's me. Stormin' Norman wants to knock us down and build a doctor's surgery."

"A doctor's surgery?"

"Yesh. His daughter is a botox surgeon."

Teresa watched Norman swat away Elsie's wandering hands. "Yeah, I don't think you've got that quite right, Ernie."

"I know what I'm talking about, Tessa," Ernie insisted, swaying from side to side. "Did you know there's a pirate ship in the Mad Pit."

Teresa shook her head and laughed. "I'd better go, Ernie. I've to photograph the Seatown men's swimming team. It's a hard life, eh?"

"All those broad shoulders," he said, stuffing a whole sausage roll into his mouth. "Like mermen.

Very piratey, Tess. Don't forget to tell Pam that Norman's evil!"

Teresa brushed spit and pastry flakes from her jacket. "I will, Ern. I'll tell her straightaway. Ta-ra."

_____ *** _____

Tristan nudged Malcolm towards the dancefloor where Louise was attempting to enforce the twenty-centimetre rule. "Go on, Mal, ask her to dance!"

"Yeah, Mal," Lupin chimed in. "Isn't 'My Ding-A-Ling' your favourite song?"

Malcolm looked completely out of his depth, more comfortable with a pair of knitting needles than on a dancefloor moving his feet in a rhythmic manner.

"I don't know, I've got three left feet," Malcolm joked, watching Louise dance with George.

"You're hilarious, Mal," Lupin said. "Isn't he hilarious, Tristan?"

"A right jokester," Tristan agreed. "Go on, lad, what have you got to lose?"

Malcolm inched towards the action. "Only my dignity; what's left of it," he muttered.

Lupin pointed at the catering table. "Tristan, please go and get me a scone. I need sustenance for this."

_____ *** _____

Bev Rogers and Stan Tweddle strolled into the library, arm in arm.

Janet was being chatted up by Councillor Nigel McKeown when her understanding of reality crashed around her twice-pierced ears. "Would you look at that," she murmured, watching the happy couple get sucked into the throng. Stan had a sturdy looking rucksack on his back. *If I know Stan, he's probably brought his own tea and sandwiches.*

"Janet, this is a wonderful event," Nigel said. "If I had my way, this place would stay open. Every town needs a library."

Janet returned her attention to Nigel. "What do you mean, 'if you had your way'?"

The elected representative shrugged. "It's simple, Janet. I'm not in the inside circle.

"I don't buy it, Nigel. All votes are equal, are they not?"

The man laughed. "Don't be naive, pet. Most of us want to do what's best for our communities. Others couldn't care less."

Janet took a large bite out of her lemon and poppyseed muffin. "Damn, that's good. Tina, one of our regulars, made that. She baked a hundred cakes for today. For free."

Nigel squirmed. "Okay?"

"Nigel, I'm not your pet. You've got a mandate, so use it to keep this place open. You know what Norman's planning, and what are you doing about it?"

"Well, now," he started, looking over Janet's head for an easy escape. "It's not that easy."

"Sweet eff all, by the sounds of things," she seethed. "Help us out here, Nigel. Ask all of the Nigels, and the handful of Nancys that can put up with you, to do their bit."

"Or what?" he asked, loosening his red tie.

"Or we'll do it for you, lad. There's a whole roomful here and hundreds more besides who can vote."

Before Councillor McKeown could respond, Janet skipped over to the dancefloor and started a conga line.

Bev and Stan were huddled together in the Children's Fiction corner. Bev was nibbling a ham and cheese triangle, Stan a crumbly caramel shortbread.

"Look at the crumbs, Stan!" Bev admonished, staring in despair at the pool of pastry gathering by their feet. "Can't you get a plate?"

"I overeat when I'm nervous, Mrs. Rogers," he admitted. "We're about to make a spectacle of ourselves. And there are no clean plates left."

"It's Bev and we both agreed to it, so eat your cake and let's go and hide."

***

No one was talking to Councillor Roach.

At last week's grand opening of the Seatown chapter of Men in Sheds, he'd insulted a selection of DIY bird boxes and joked that older gents should still be working instead of drinking coffee and gossiping like a bunch of women.

He shouldn't be here at all. Being in the same room as Ernie Noble was a risk. What he wanted to do was make a great show of exposing his home invader but then he'd have to reveal himself as a thief. What worked in his favour, however, was the fact that Ernie was drunk and dressed like a Bavarian go-go dancer.

Unused to being ignored, Norman quietly slipped away.

***

'The Seatown Swingers' was at the encore stage of a long and testing set. They'd refused any further requests after playing 'Delilah' four times, and the bass player had to coach junior footie at seven o'clock, so a speedy finish was in order.

The singer grabbed his mic. "Ladies and gentleman, it's been our absolute pleasure supporting the Madeleine Pit Library this evening. We'll leave you with this little gem, 'Paperback Writer."

"Read more books! 1, 2, 3, 4!" yelled the drummer, before launching into the Beatles classic.

"Did you choose this cupboard so you could molest me, woman?" Stan asked, spitting Bev's hair from his mouth.

"No, silly," Bev shot back. "This is Maeve's cupboard. *No one* goes in here but her."

"So we're safe?"

"Yes, so stay still and keep your hands to yourself."

Stan sucked in his stomach. "I'm keeping as far away from you as I possibly can, woman."

***

The staff team, plus Courtney, swept up and rearranged the library floor until it looked like sixty debauched pensioners hadn't tried to pound the colour out of the carpet tiles.

"That was great crack," Lupin said, flinging herself onto a soft chair. "Councillor McKeown was coming on to you, Janet."

"Give over," Janet laughed. "Pete, put the kettle on. I need to tell you all something."

Pete and Courtney exchanged a worried glance.

***

Courtney licked vanilla frosting from her fingers. "Tell me I'm thick, yeah, but how is this grotty piece of paper going to keep the Pit open?"

Janet counted to five in her head. "Love, we've just read it three times. It's the covenant mentioned in those meeting minutes. It basically says that by law, the library has to remain open."

"Right, so that piece of paper *is* the treasure?"

Yes," said Tristan. "Unless there are diamonds and rubies buried under the garage, obviously."

"I'm knackered, Tristan," Courtney warned. "Don't encourage me to take a swing at you."

Janet yawned and stretched her arms above her head. "We've had a long day."

Lupin put the last of the clean crockery in the cupboard. "We'll have to show it to a solicitor. One that's not in the council's pocket."

"I know a decent one," Tristan offered. "My mother's used her for her last three divorces."

"I hope it works," Pete said, scrubbing lipstick from his cheek with a wet tea towel. "I really don't want to have to move to the Highways Depot."

Tristan pointed to Pete's face. "You picked up a few extra fans today, lad."

"That's why he doesn't want to move to Highways," Courtney mocked. "No little old ladies there to worship him."

Janet stood up and surveyed the library floor. "Alright, everything looks decent. Maeve won't have too much to do in the morning."

Chapter Forty

"What if we have to use the loo, Stan?" Bev asked, pressing down on her bladder. "I had four coffees at that tea dance."

Stan pulled a length of chain from his backpack. "Ms. Rogers, I'd suggest you go to the toilet now before we chain ourselves to Janet's desk."

"I can't, silly," she groaned. "The loo's downstairs and I heard them set the alarm before they left. We didn't think this through, did we?"

The duo looked at each other and then at Janet's waste paper bin. "Stan, desperate times call for desperate measures. Close your eyes and ears."

"Oh no, you don't," Stan said. "I haven't listened to a woman urinate since nineteen ninty-eight."

Bev upended the bin and emptied its contents onto the floor. "And what, pray, were you doing in nineteen ninety-eight, Stan?"

"You've got a filthy mind, woman," he said. "I was camping with Sheila at Wastwater, if you must know."

"You never talk about Sheila," she noted. "We were great pals."

"I know," he said, dropping his head.

"Right, shut your eyes and sing a little tune, Stan. I'm bursting here."

Stan walked to the far side of the office and screwed his eyes shut.

"Ears too, lad! There'll be quite a stream."

Stan sighed. *What is it with this place and indiscriminate urination?*

"You know," he said. "We don't have to chain ourselves right away. I'll get my torch out and read the paper, over here. You can do whatever you want. Over there."

Bev pulled up her tracksuit bottoms. "Whatever you want, Stan."

***

Norman was used to members-only bars. The golf club. The rugby club. Salubrious establishments where you made a show of spending twenty quid on an insipid bottle of red.

He knew where he stood in those places.

This pub smelled damp and was full of dusty old knick knacks. *Lesley would have a fit in here.*

He climbed onto a bar stool and knocked on the bar top. "Double Laphroaig."

The barman turned his back to make up the order. "We've got a special on scampi fries. They're out of date."

"Alright then, gimme two bags."

A gang of brightly dressed young people congregated in one corner, nursing orange alcopops and laughing at nothing in particular. In the other, a handful of ruddy faced middle-aged men drained pints of locally brewed ale in companionable silence. Both factions were trying to eavesdrop on the other.

"Busy night?" Norman drawled.

"Pretty average," the barman replied. "Next weekend will be a different story."

"How's that?"

"Pay day," the man said, as if the answer was obvious.

"Right. Another whisky. Please." Sometimes he forgot to be polite, until he remembered camera phones existed and that the adults of Seatown could vote.

***

"I told you my furry handcuffs would come in handy, Stan," Bev laughed, rattling them from her corner of Janet's office.

"I hope they've been thoroughly sanitised," Stan said, without looking up from his paper.

Bev winked. "A dose of dettol every time I use them."

She returned to the Danielle Steele balancing on her thighs. "It's not often I get the time to read like this," she said, adjusting her reading light.

Stan turned the page a little too briskly. "Too busy canoodling with your toy boys, I expect."

"No, silly. Looking after my grandbabies."

"How's your Adele doing?" Stan asked, reluctant to get drawn into a conversation. "In under ten words, if you don't mind."

"Very well, still married, boys are bouncing," she replied, counting her fingers.

"That's good."

"Aye."

_____ *** _____

Whiskey made Norman sweat.

He steadied himself. *One wrong move and I'll slip off this bar stool. Cheap PVC.* He looked over at the young drinkers, one of whom was waving a phone about. *They just want people like me to fall over so they can post it on Face Crack. Oh no, I'm not representing Seatown Council in an appropriate manner. I'm in trouble.*

"Did you just say something?" the barman asked.

"No, lad, not me. Top me up, will you?"

Dave, for that was the barman's name, if Norman had bothered to ask, was ready to cut him off. "Last one, eh?"

"Make it a triple then."

Dave checked his watch. Last orders had passed so he'd be out of here soon. Home to a pepperoni pizza and his pomeranian, Dizzy.

"Coming up."

_____ *** _____

Bev tiptoed over to the snoring man in the corner and discreetly opened his rucksack. She pulled out a fleece blanket and draped it over him.

Back in her half of the office, she checked her phone. *Eleven o'clock. That's my longest reading streak in a long while. If his nibs stays asleep I'll maybe get this one finished; I need to know what happens to the stable hand.*

Chapter Forty One

Norman had a plan.

"I'm making an executive decision," he told Dave, who was wiping down the bar top. "When something needs done, you've got to do it yourself."

"Are you going to do it outside?" Dave asked, pointedly looking at the door. "I need to get home to my dog."

A dog's not going to dig up the library. I need heavy machinery.

_____ *** _____

Norman stumbled out of the 'Drunken Sailor' and vomited onto a Honda Civic.

Wiping his mouth with the back of his hand, he shuffled up to a lamp post and rested his head against it. "Ask for forgiveness, not permission."

He pointed himself towards Seatown Industrial Estate and started walking.

_____ *** _____

Stan's snoring woke him. Rubbing his eyes, he briefly panicked before clocking Bev curled up on the floor using her Danielle Steele as a pillow.

He unfurled himself from the fleece with a quiet groan. *I really need to relieve myself.*

The bucket taunted him from its dim corner. Never had Stan imagined he'd empty his bladder beside a woman like Bev Rogers. *How the mighty have fallen.*

_____ *** _____

One step forward, two steps back, Norman was making unsteady progress to the industrial estate.

At its grassy entrance he bent to pet a guinea pig before realising it was a dead rat. *That was disappointing. I wonder if Lesley would like a pet rat. I could take this one home with me but my pockets aren't deep enough.*

As the gates to Jenkins Plant Hire loomed into view, Norman's stream of mumbling came to a halt.

"The time to act is now," he boomed, taking a set of keys from his coat pocket.

What Seatown Council didn't know was that Norman's brother-in-law, Dan, owned a plant hire company. Once, after a nightmare where Janine had dressed as a fairy and set fire to the Mad Pit, Norman had pinched Dan's keys and made copies. He recognised that the day might come when desperate measures would have to be taken.

Tonight was that day.

***

"Stan Tweddle, you're cheating!" Bev shrieked, using her feet to propel the swivel chair around the stuffed donkey. "You're supposed to race *around* the farm animals, not over them."

Stan bent over and picked up the fluffy animal. "Your trainers have got grip, woman! I'm wearing brogues. We're not competing on equal terms."

Bev glanced at her watch. "It's half-twelve. I suppose we're due another nap."

"Maybe have one more round, eh?"

"Oh, go on then."

***

Norman walked over the gravel and approached a lone portaloo. "I want the biggest wrecking ball you've got, good sir."

Half a minute lapsed and, offended at the despicable service, Norman decided to take matters into his own hands.

"You can't get the staff," he muttered, throwing off his jacket and jogging towards the back of the plant. "Paying 'em too much."

The keys fell out of his hand. "Oopsie."

He picked them up and, after a few failed attempts and some swearing, the heavy machinery gate clicked open.

_____ *** _____

Constables O'Neill and Hamilton cruised along Main Street, openly frustrated at the lack of Friday night tomfoolery. The radio was quiet and the pubs had spat out fairly well behaved punters.

"Let's take a bimble up Cutters," Michelle suggested, executing a yawn that flashed every filling. "Then we can stop at Maccy D's for a coffee."

"Go for it," agreed Jack. "But you're going into Maccy's."

"Yeah, yeah."

_____ *** _____

Norman had never operated a hydraulic excavator but he reckoned it couldn't be any harder than driving a Land Rover.

"Come on then, you big giraffe," he bellowed into the night sky. "Bark at the mooooon!"

Then there were two hydraulic excavators.

He shook his head and blinked. "Ah, just the one."

The next fly in the ointment was getting into the cab. Norman looked around the site, spotted a bench and dragged it over to the machine. "Bingo."

He opened the cab door and hoisted himself inside. The key was in the ignition. *It's like a funfair, only better. 'Cos instead of winning a cuddly toy I'm going to break that library into a million little pieces.*

Sliding the seat forward, his feet barely tapped the pedals.

He turned the key.

Somewhere in the far reaches of his pickled mind he remembered Dan once telling him that the engine needed time to warm up.

He decided to give it thirty seconds.

———————— *** ————————

"Weeeeeee!"

Norman was having the time of this life. No pussy footing around public servants here.

He was in charge. He was the King of Seatown.

He aimed his invisible sword at the exit. "To the palace of stupid books, my fine yellow steed!"

The main road to town was in his sights. All he needed to do was keep this beast moving in a straight line. Easy peasy.

Before he could proceed, pretty, flashing colours lit up the sky. *Janine and her fairy friends are coming to help! With their fat cheeks and big eyebrows!*

Ear-splitting noise filled the air. *"Sir, please switch off the, em, machine and step out of the cab with your hands above your head."*

"Hush, would you? I've got a whisky headache! And they're the worst kind!"

Norman was no longer convinced that fairies existed. *It's the filth.*

"Sir, we're coming in. Raise your hands where we can see them."

***

"Am I low in caffeine or is there a digger coming out of the industrial estate?"

Jack shook his head. "No, there is definitely something coming out, and whoever's driving it is either having a stroke or they're pissed as a fart."

"We're going to need backup." Michelle called it in.

The pair parked up on a layby and made tentative steps towards the vehicle.

"There's a coat lying on the ground," Jack said, picking it up. "It's a tacky old man sport's jacket and it stinks of scampi fries."

"That's evidence!" Michelle shouted, ducking out of the way of the oncoming boom.

He pulled a driving licence from the inside pocket and peered at it. "Oh my days, this has made my life!"

"What?"

Jack held up the licence. "It's only Councillor Norman Cockroach!"

"Think of the paperwork," Michelle groaned, squinting up at the cab. "If we both blink at the same time do you think we'll be in Maccy's when we open our eyes?"

"Nope," Jack sighed. Norman had started to warble Queen's seminal hit, 'Don't Stop Me Now'. "Come on, Freddie Mercury needs arresting."

***

"Thank God you're here, Inspector," Norman cried, jiggling the joy stick. "I need you to close the gate after me, otherwise Dan'll have a fit."

The excavator boom started a slow dance.

The officers crouched in stereo. "This is Constable Hamilton and I'm Constable O'Neill," Michelle yelled over the rumbling engine."We need you to turn off the engine, get down out of the cab and come with us."

"Put your hands above your head," Jack shouted. *I think the German term for this warm, fuzzy feeling is Schadenfreude.* "Say 'I'm a bent politician' if you don't understand."   .

"What was that, son? Do you know I am?"

"Sadly, yes," Jack muttered.

Norman did everyone a favour and tumbled out of the cab.

"Ow."

———————— *** ————————

Out of the corner of his eyes, Stan watched Bev brush her silvery grey hair. *For a jezebel she has very well conditioned locks.*

"What eyeshadow do you think would suit me, Stan?" she asked.

"I would stick to light neutrals, lass."

Bev nodded. "Yes, I thought so. You know, you should take up Avon again."

"No, never. I wouldn't have time to write my letters, would I?"

The pair looked at each other and laughed.

Bev set down her brush. "Time for another cuppa?"

"Let's break out the biscuits too," Stan said, opening a container of broken bourbon creams.

"Ooh, you're spoiling us. Are they from the middle aisle?"

"Where else, Bev?" he joked, holding a chunk aloft. "The perfect protest sweet treat. Hardy and not too tasty."

Yes, we don't want to get lost in chocolate that's *too* heavenly," Bev agreed, biting into one.

"Never forget why we're doing what we're doing."

After a spot of quiet munching, Bev felt they'd been there long enough for an honest conversation.

"Stan?

"Yes?"

"While we're here why don't we, you know, have a look around?

Stan brushed crumbs from his lap. "Look around?"

"This is a big office," she said, picking up a sheaf of paper from Janet's desk and flicking through it. "There's got to be summat juicy. But not these. These are nursery rhymes."

"You're bored."

"So bored."

"Alright then. Where do you want to start?"

Bev smiled. "Well, Janet has got to have a lipstick drawer. Why don't we look for that?"

Stan rolled up his shirt sleeves. "It's in the public interest, I suppose."

***

Norman struggled to remember how he'd ended up in the back of a taxi.

"I haven't given you my address," he croaked at the partition. "How will you know where to drop me off?"

Michelle and Jack turned to look at each other. "You're coming to ours for the after party, Councillor."

***

"Now this is a good quality matte lipstick," Stan declared, holding a golden tube aloft. "Peach really complements Janet's light skin tone."

Bev was agog. "Your talents are wasted on being angry, Stan."

The pair had ransacked every drawer, which only left the filing cabinet. "There's no key in it, Stan. It's like an open invitation."

Stan pulled out the bottom drawer. "The weird stuff is always in the bottom drawer.

"Yeah, the stuff there's no divider for," Bev agreed, clocking a cotton shopper resting between bags of mixed fruit chews. "Like these duty free sweets."

"And that shopping bag," Stan added. "What's in it?"

Bev cleared some space and placed the bag on Janet's desk. "You do the honours, Stan and I'll point my reading light at it."

The second he opened it all of Stan's dreams came true at once. "I knew it! Do you know what this is, Bev?"

She turned her nose up at the miniature ship. "Some middle-aged man's excuse for a hobby?"

"No," he breathed, gently nursing the boat in his hands. "This is an old model of 'The King's Maiden.'"

"How do you know that?"

Stan carefully placed the ship on Janet's desk. "When I was a kid, no one liked me."

Bev had the decency to look shocked. "I don't believe that for a second, a friendly lad like you."

302

"I was an only child," Stan continued. "And not into rugby or football."

"Which left?"

"Model ships."

"Obviously."

Stan looked at the ship. "This little beauty was a naval ship until the pirates took it for themselves."

"Pirates? Around here?" Bev shook her head. "I doubt it. Maybe you've got it mixed up with, I dunno, Cornwall."

Stan sat back on his chair and put his hands behind his head. "It all makes sense. I knew I'd heard Janet and that team of rag tags talking about treasure a few weeks back."

"Why is it here?" Bev asked, wishing she was back in the stable with her muscled horse boy.

Stan looked up at her. "Like I said, I didn't really have friends. So, I spent a lot of time with my grandmother, Irene."

"Oh, that's nice," Bev said, trying not to feel sorry for the man.

"I'd call in after school. By that stage she'd be on her fifth sherry."

"Whose gran doesn't like sherry, eh?" she laughed, reaching into the box of broken biscuits and handing him one.

"Thanks. My other nana was teetotal."

"Yeah, fair enough. Go on."

Stan settled into his role as storyteller. "She'd start talking about pirates, you see. Tales of criminals running riot through Seatown. But these pirates, they came from all over, and they quickly came to realise that Seatown was the perfect place to smuggle in and stash their ill-gotten gains."

"This is all very Dickensian," Bev admitted. "I've never heard anything about pirates in Seatown. Are you sure your gran wasn't just feeding you a tall tale?"

He shook his head. "She might have been a borderline alcoholic but she was no liar. Her brutal honesty lost her many friends."

"You don't say," Bev grinned. *The apple didn't fall far from the sherry tree.* "Go on."

"The King's Maiden escorted slave ships. That was until our gang of thieves jumped on board back in seventeen hundred and frozen stiff and well, hijacked it. It was a bloodbath, and with the proceeds they set up shop here and invited their friends. Some of them even settled and had families."

Bev was confused. "So, Seatown was like a holiday resort for crims?"

"I suppose it was." There was a pause. "Until the people rose up."

He raised his eyebrows, enjoying Bev's look of bewilderment.

"They what? Seatown people? The most apathetic town in England?"

"No, that's where you're absolutely wrong, Bev. You should know better," he scolded. "How much have you raised from this 'uncaring' community?"

Bev bit into another bourbon. "Okay, fair enough, oh, wise man of the sea."

"The community came together and ran those bad lads out of town!" Stan exclaimed, warming to his subject. "Pitchforks may have been involved, who knows? My grandmother liked to finish this story on a child-friendly note."

"Again, what the Charles Dickens has this boat got to do with anything?" Bev asked, glancing at the ship.

Stan's shoulders slumped. "It's not my model. This one is quite old, indeed."

"Then why is this itty bitty boat in Janet's filing cabinet?"

"I don't know."

"And how come I've never heard of this piracy?"

Stan laughed bitterly. "Because it's embarrassing, woman. Who wants to admit that their town was the home of criminals and people traders? And people do know. We just don't talk about it."

Bev yawned. "Maybe we need to focus on the good people of Seatown. They're the ones that won, after all."

Stan smiled. "You're right, for once."

"It happens more than you think," she winked.

Streaks of morning light penetrated the window, illuminating 'The King's Maiden' and Stan's undereye bags. "Stan, you need a couple of night's sleep," Bev chuckled.

"I need to figure out this model ship. It's hardly treasure."

Bev picked up her furry handcuffs. "Stanley Tweddle, it's time we chained ourselves to Janet's desk."

Chapter Forty Two

Maeve parked her Micra outside the Mad Pit. Having her pick of town centre parking spaces at five in the morning would never grow old.

After knocking off the alarm, she made her way to the cleaning cupboard and opened the door. *It smells like mothballs and Impulse Musk in here.*

Moving up the stairs she heard what sounded like the clanking of chains echoing from Janet's office. "I'm not afraid of you, Jacob Marley," she yelled, dropping the bucket and brandishing her mop. "Gird your loins, ghost!"

Ghost or not, Maeve had never backed down from a fight.

The trail of musk led her into the office which is where she figured out the how, but not the why.

"Am I interrupting some weird kind of sado-masochistic roleplay between two people that hate each other?" she asked. "Because I've got dusting to do."

Bev lifted her handcuffed wrist and rattled the chain that connected her and Stan to Janet's desk leg. "I don't know what kind of kinky games you engage in, Maeve, but this ain't one."

"My leg's dead," Stan complained, rubbing his thigh with his free hand. "This is not fun for me."

Maeve leaned her mop against the wall. "Let me guess, this is a protest?"

"Yes, love," Bev said. "You know, I'm glad you're here, because I've left the key to our handcuffs in my bag."

Stan's face broke out in a sweat. "You did what?"

"Now, Stan, don't go ruining our good vibe," Bev joked. "You've witnessed many protests then, doll?"

Maeve casually waved her hand. "One or two. Greenham, Porton Down. No arrests."

"You're a proper protest professional, are you?" Stan mocked. "Well, don't for a minute think that we're amateurs. We've been here all night."

"You do you, love," Maeve said, pulling a duster from her pocket. "I need to get on with my cleaning."

Before she could attack Janet's disgusting keyboard, her eyes lit on the boat. "What's this doing here?"

"We're pointed in the wrong direction," Bev said, from her vantage point on the floor. "Are you talking about the boat or the fourteen lipsticks we lined up on her desk?"

"We put them in order of most to least flattering," piped up Stan.

"Yes, the boat," Maeve groaned, spraying polish onto the keys.

"Well, don't tell Janet but we got bored and decided to have a little rummage," Bev admitted.

Maeve threw her head back and laughed. "You didn't think to put it back before you put on your handcuffs?"

"No," the prisoners said in unison.

Maeve wiped around the boat. "It's just as well I'm the cleaner then, isn't it? Once I finish up here I'll put it back."

"Mum's the word?" Bev asked.

"Mum's the word, pet," Maeve confirmed, leaving the office. "Good luck and don't think about water otherwise you'll need to pee."

"Harlot!" Stan spat.

_____ *** _____

Maeve laughed all the way back to her car.

She pulled on her seat belt, started the engine and turned on the radio.

"Reports have just emerged that Seatown Council elected member, Councillor Norman Roach, has been arrested for trespassing in the Seatown Industrial Estate and attempting to operate heavy machinery

under the influence and without a licence. Further details will be forthcoming. Now, over to Debbie for the farming weather…"

A broad grin spread across her face. *Sometimes justice is the greatest gift of all.*

She opened her glove compartment and found her Queen Greatest Hits CD. *Hmm, 'Another One Bites The Dust,' I think.*

——————— *** ———————

Bev and Stan spent the next two hours playing 'I Spy,' which was a struggle considering the only things in the room were books, office furniture and a bucket full of pee.

Bev scratched her ankle with her free hand. "Stan, love?"

"Aye?"

"What time are Gavin and Teresa coming?"

Stan pulled a face. "Ha ha."

"Don't joke, Stan," Bev snarled. "My bladder is *very* full and I didn't pack my Tena."

Stan covered his left ear with his free hand. "No, no, no. I didn't need to hear that."

"What time are they coming?"

"You booked them, woman, you tell me!" Stan said, eyes bulging.

"Ooh, I didn't!" she yelped, crossing her legs. "What'll we do!"

"What'll *who* do?" Janet said, stepping into her office. "Can I help? You're both handcuffed to my desk. So basically, this is just a normal Saturday morning."

The captives froze.

"Be a pet and ask Teresa and Gavin to come here and photograph us," Bev asked, sweetly. "We're not very organised, are we?"

Janet walked around them and sat in her chair. "This chair feels warm. Were you having races?"

Stan sniffed. "Maybe."

"Can you ask them to come as soon as they can, Janet? We're both busting here."

"So you were only going to stay locked up until you had your photo taken?" Janet asked. "Not much of a hardship, is it?"

Stan frowned. "You make a good point, Janet. How about you ring the paper, uncuff us so we can use the loo, then lock us up again?"

"You geriatrics and your weak bladders."

"Janet!" Bev laughed. "I'm wee-ing myself!"

Gavin scribbled into his notebook. "And how are you going to manage the toilet situation?"

A blushing Stan gave Bev the nod. "Well," she started. "We're taking regular breaks for that, Gavin, because, as you know, people of our age can't mess with nature. We have a bucket but hoping that now Janet's here she'll allow us to use the library loo. We're also uncuffing ourselves once an hour for a couple of laps to avoid deep vein thrombosis."

"What does Janet say about this awareness raising stunt?"

"Janet thinks it's very commendable but Janet can't work and watch people urinate at the same time," Janet barked from behind her computer, typing furiously. "So Janet's emailing the insurance company for clarification."

Gavin tried not to laugh. "Bev, what are you trying to achieve by this?"

Bev rattled her end of the chain. "Isn't it obvious?"

"I just need a usable quote," Gavin said.

"Oh, okay," she said. "How about this: 'Stan and I, among many other Seatown residents, are passionate supporters of the Mad Pit...'"

"Madeleine Pit," Stan interjected.

"Yes," Bev snapped, shooting Stan a glance. "Look, Gavin, we love this library. We came here as kids to do our homework. Stan's read every world war two biography ever written…"

Stan nodded.

"…Jackie Collins, God rest her fabulous soul, got me through my post-natal depression. My grandkids have sung and danced here. They've learned here. Our older community meets here for craft and a crack. It's warm, welcoming and you couldn't ask for a kinder or more efficient staff team."

Stan raised his free hand. "The computer suite gives me my voice, Gavin."

Gavin felt that the last thing the computer suite needed was Stan and his one-fingered typing but he stayed silent, pen poised, ever the professional.

"Yes, Stan is a pest but that's his right, isn't it, Gav?" Bev smiled, encouragingly.

Stan had lost all feeling in his bottom. "Not so much a pest, as a concerned citizen keeping local government accountable."

Bev gazed at Stan's lower half. "I think we need to hurry this up, Stan's getting pins and needles."

"'Cumbria Press Photographer of 2012' has arrived." Teresa barged in through the open doorway. "Well, then. This has been the most entertaining Saturday morning I've had in a while."

Janet looked up from her keyboard. "What, you mean you've never seen two sworn enemies handcuffed together in a municipal building before?"

"Sadly no," Teresa said, removing her camera from its padded bag. "I'm raging I wasn't loitering by the industrial estate last night."

"Why's that?" Janet asked, pressing send on her email.

"You mean, you haven't heard about the shenanigans?" Teresa asked, pointing her camera at Janet's confused expression.

"What shenanigans?" Stan's buttocks were in agony.

"I'm not good at Saturday shifts," Janet admitted, blushing at the memory of driving to the end of the street in her slippers this morning. "I haven't had time to check the news."

"Norman Roach has been arrested," Teresa announced, with great satisfaction.

"What?" Janet wondered if she was still in bed, dreaming. "How? Why?"

"For being drunk in charge of a digger," Gavin said. "Apparently he was babbling about demolishing the Pit."

Janet wished her team was here to witness this, but life didn't work that way. She had to make her move. "Maybe it's time to tell you all about the boat."

"What boat?" Stan asked, innocently.

***

By the time Janet had finished, Bev and Stan had had two toilet breaks, Lupin had arrived to tell her family's side of the story and Tristan was outlining his tell-all book.

"It all makes sense now," Teresa said, taking a sip of coffee. "Ernie was going on about pirates and mermen yesterday. I just assumed it was because he was drunk."

Stan tutted. "Typical Ernie, no self-respect."

"I thought his hot pants were cutting the oxygen off to his brain," Tristan laughed, his mouth full of custard tart.

"Who's downstairs on the floor?" Lupin asked Janet.

"Pete is, and he's not happy. There's been a rush of tweens."

Bev looked at Stan. "Do you think we should *all* go downstairs?

Stan exhaled heavily. "Yes please, but someone's going to have to carry me. Both my legs are dead now."

"There's a job for you, Tristan," Janet said, looking down at the pair. "And don't think I've forgotten what you two reprobates have done. We'll have to check every room and cupboard before we lock up now, thanks to you."

***

Ernie flounced into the library, still clad in his pleather hot pants. "Pete, lad, I need you to go to Watson's chemist and get me some talcum powder."

Pete was checking out the Pit's stock of Suzanne Collins to a clique of Katniss Everdeen look-alikes. "Ernie, I'm busy." Then he looked up. "Ernie, please hide."

As Ernie and his pants slithered behind the DVDs, another badly dressed member of the community stormed in.

"Give me the heads of Janet Sowerpuss, Lupin 'the pirate' Lawson and Tristan Apple!" demanded Councillor Norman Roach, clutching a bottle of summer fruits cider.

"It's Pear, you daft crook."

Norman swung around, teetering on his heels. "Who said that?"

316

Ernie emerged from his hiding place. "I did, you poor excuse for a human."

Norman stared at Ernie's crotch. "Are you auditioning for the Sound of Music, Klaus?"

"That's racist!"

Pete herded the snickering preteens out of the side door and cautiously approached the men.

"Can you move this outside, please? You're scaring the books."

Ernie laughed. "You know, Pete, your sense of humour has really come on in the last few months."

Norman grabbed Ernie's brushed cotton pyjama top. "Did you just get out of bed, hobo?"

A bright flash forced all three to turn and look up.

As Teresa snapped, Janet clapped. "Does anyone else feel like it's their birthday?"

Ernie squinted at the slack-jawed spectators. "Is there cake?"

Norman ran towards the stairs, but before he could gain a foothold, Ernie rugby tackled him in one smooth motion. "Like my shorts now, lad? Do you want to wear them?"

"Get off me, Noble," Norman cried, wriggling out of Ernie's grasp. "This is MY building."

Gavin skipped down the stairs with his notebook and pen. "Councillor Roach, can you comment on why you were behind the wheel of a hydraulic excavator in the early hours of this morning?"

Norman belched fruity fumes over Gavin's appalled face. "Can't a man engage in a little town modelling when he wants to?"

"Well, no. Obviously."

A flood of purple vomit drenched Gavin's trainers. "Howzat, hack," Norman jabbered, wiping his mouth. "Anyone else fancy a warm cider?"

Pete backed away from the steaming puke. "We'll have no carpet tiles left at this rate."

As Pete dashed to the kitchen for a cloth, Janet and Lupin linked arms and descended the staircase.

Lupin released her witchiest war cry. "On three, charge!"

Within seconds the great Norman Roach had been toppled by two angry women and restrained by a hot pant wearing pensioner.

"Get off me, man!" Norman roared, trying to wrestle himself out of Ernie's grip. "I know you broke into my bungalow!"

Tristan was bent over double with laughter. "What's he on about, Ernie? I can't handle this," he wheezed.

"He's drunk, don't listen to him," Ernie said. "Help me out here, Tricia, I'm very slippery in these pants."

Tristan pulled a piece of paper from his back pocket. "You'll need to hold still for another minute Ernie, then we'll get you some talc."

Norman twisted his head. "Talc?"

"Take a look at this, Councillor Cockroach." Tristan got down on his knees, unfolded the sheet of paper and waved it in front of Norman's face. "This is a legal document."

Norman blew a raspberry, covering the sheet in drool. "Do I look like a lawyer, Mr. Soft Fruit?"

"It was written over two hundred years ago by good people who ran bad people out of Seatown. Pirates. Criminals. Politicians like you, Norm."

"Excuse me?"

"Yes, bad people like you," Tristan continued. "This legal covenant states that Seatown will have a library. This building cannot be demolished, no matter how important your childhood dream of operating an excavator under the influence of whisky was."

"Or how much your spoiled daughter *really* needs another botox clinic under her fake Chanel belt," Lupin crowed, kicking Norman with a purple suede boot.

"Lupin, you can't kick him!" Janet said, pulling her by the arm. "Just, you know, spit on him when no-one else is looking."

A now shoeless Gavin pulled Teresa towards the ringside seats. "You'd pay a fortune for this kind of entertainment at Civic Hall," Teresa noted, settling into a reading armchair, camera armed and ready.

While Norman was reaching up to grab the document, a stiff Bev and Stan joined the party, sans chains and handcuffs.

"You think I'd let you see the real thing?" Tristan mocked, snatching the paper away from the Councillor's grasping fingers. "This is a photocopy."

Stan gasped. "That machine is actually working for once?"

***

After Norman had been hauled away by the police for the second time in twenty-four hours, the extended Mad Pit staff and supporters shut up shop and gathered together for a good old-fashioned library lock-in, with rounds of coffee and cake replacing warm beer and stale scampi fries.

Gavin and Teresa had reluctantly moved on to their next job, despite a burning desire to continue the festivities at *Chez Mad Pit*. They were satisfied with their golden scoop, however, and left proceedings confident of a nod at the annual regional media awards.

Come late afternoon, the fizzing energy of that morning had dampened down to a manageable camaraderie that permitted even Stan and Ernie to find common ground.

"What I want to know is where that boat came from," Janet said, tearing half of her chocolate eclair and handing it to Lupin.

"Why didn't you say, lass?" Ernie asked, lying across three chairs. "I could have told you that."

"I already asked you and you played dumb!"

Ernie sat up. He'd managed to extricate himself from the pleather and was sporting a pair of aged ten navy jogging bottoms recovered from the lost and found box. "I couldn't say anything in front of the crafters."

"Why ever not?" Lupin inquired, her mouth full of choux pastry. "It's not like you to hold back, Ernie."

Ernie briefly considered if Stan would tell tales, then decided to be bold and confess.

"Well, it all started with that box of paper and ended with me breaking into Norman's house dressed as Postman Pat."

Epilogue

"Where are the buggering mayoral scissors?"

Lupin was panicking. Today was a big day. Today she was going to be proud to be a Lawson.

"What the heck are mayoral scissors?" Courtney asked, as she and Pete were unfurling a long silky strip of royal blue ribbon across the library floor.

Janet emerged from the kitchen serene in top to toe red, wearing a striking scarlet lip gloss. Her blonde bob was hurricane-proof and her mood was buoyant.

"Try not to panic, Lupin, but we don't have any." Janet ran her finger along the top of the enlarged framed Seatown library covenant. *No dust. Good on you, Maeve Mills, saver of libraries, queen of Seatown, beloved pillar of the community.* At the bottom of the covenant was a list of signatories, two of which were Lawson and Mills.

Leaning against the new 'Seatown's Storied Past' display, Lupin closed her eyes and tried to visualise her spirit owl, but it was dodging her mind's eye. "Then how is the mayor supposed to cut the ribbon?"

Tristan finished straightening out Museum Corner. "We really need a more swashbuckling name for our pirate museum."

"Ask Ernie?" Pete suggested.

"Ask Ernie what?" the man said, striding into the library in a brown pinstripe suit with flared trousers. "Do you like my get up?" He did a twirl. "I found it in a skip."

Janet blanched. "You did not!"

"Nah. Philip from the funeral home gave it to me. Apparently it was old Mr. Johnston's backup choice."

No one quite knew how to respond.

"So, what do you need?"

"A big, shiny pair of scissors fit for a mayor," Tristan replied.

***

Janet surveyed the library floor: a room full of happy people and not an out of date Mr. Kipling in sight.

Hazel, Maeve and Pauline were huddled in the corner, enthusiastically deconstructing Norman Roach's fall from grace. "What are you going to do with yourself now, Maeve?" asked Pauline. "You know, now that Seatown's reputation has been temporarily restored?"

"What do you mean, 'temporarily'?" Maeve joked. "Are you predicting future scandals?"

Pauline rolled her eyes. "There's always a Norman or Norma, ladies."

Violet and her crafters guided visitors around, flaunting their recently completed 'History of Seatown' tapestry, replete with pirates and pitchforks. When they weren't doing that, they were forcing Tina's bundt cake on anyone with two hands and a mouth.

Resplendent in her chains and a natty lilac trouser suit, Mayor Susan Mackay stepped up to the lectern and tapped the mic. "Ladies and gentlemen, may I have your attention please?"

Stan and Bev glared at anyone still daring to chatter.

"Welcome to the opening of 'The Seatown Covenant' permanent display and museum, here at the Madeleine Pit Library," she began, zeroing in on the man in the seventies suit. "I am delighted to see that this proud period of our history is finally seeing the light of day." She gestured to the framed covenant. "I'm also thrilled to announce that our beloved Pit will remain open for the foreseeable future."

Courtney and Pete each held an end of the ribbon. It was pulled taut across a large glass case that housed a selection of historical items donated by residents, all of whom were happy and willing to confront the good and the bad of Seatown.

"The scissors!" exclaimed a red-faced Lupin, bursting through a group of dignitaries.

"Not to worry, lass," Ernie said, as he approached the Mayor with his hand extended. "I found these nail clippers in this dead chap's jacket pocket. Will they do?"

The End

Printed in Great Britain
by Amazon